OAK MOON

THE GODDESS CHRONICLES BOOK 5

KB ANNE

Published August 2020

Published by Gripping Tales, LLC, Pennsylvania.

ISBN: 978-1-956915-04-4

Cover Design by Anika Willmans, Ravenborn Covers

Editorial Services by Laura Parnum, Laura Parnum Books

❀ Created with Vellum

To Kylie,
My Number One Fan
and My Creative Soul

JOIN THE KOVEN

Read Clarissa and Carman's origin story, The Druids Sisters of the Gallicennial, FREE by signing up for K's Koven. Be the FIRST to find out about new releases from Best-Selling Author, K.B. Anne. PLUS, receive Newsletter Subscriber Only Bonus Content, insight on Celtic Mythology, Druids, Witches, Werewolves, and Magic, and so much more! Join K's Koven today!

PORTAL RIPPER

*P*ortal hopping takes some getting used to. It literally rips your innards out of your throat and shoves them down your gullet before you land. Sorta like a hangover after an especially overindulgent alcohol-fueled night—not that I've had any of those recently, what with Alaric missing and all, but holy gods, I'm back on my planet Earth. Well, I guess Scott and I never technically left the planet, if what Gallean told us about the Land of Shadows being a part of the Earthly Realm is true. Who am I to argue with the old wizard anyway? The layers of maps he showed us in his study were difficult to dispute. The gods know I searched for an opportunity to argue and couldn't find one.

The Shadow Realm certainly felt like we were in another dimension. Definitely a different time period. I expected knights with shining metal armor to rap their fists upon Gallean's carved wooden door and declare us all witches and threaten to burn us at the stake.

Thankfully we didn't land in Salem, Massachusetts in the 1700s or medieval Europe when witch burners ran rampant and took sadistic pleasure in discovering new methods of torture. Some people need to find better ways to get over their sexual repression. They're lucky I wasn't around then, or I would have shown them just how hot fire can get. I might not be able to harm another living being, but as far as I know there's no manual that states I can't douse them in gasoline and light a match. But alas, I digress.

If the Shadow Realm's curtain of magical mist continues to lift, the world will know about the island, and if today's populations get their environment-killing hands on it, the timeless beauty will be destroyed along with Gallean, his keep, and all the townspeople. Our modern world would probably call them heretics and burn them at the stake.

But then again, the revelation of a newly discovered island might not rank high on the Top 10 New Places to Destroy, because if the Fomorians are released, everyone in the world will either become their slave or die. Not exactly a win-win situation, if you ask me.

To be honest, I'm a little freaked out. Actually, I'm a lot of freaked out. But at least I'm back in Kildare, and I know how to find my way home from the fairy mound. I could do that in my sleep. And thus far, I haven't been attacked by a werewolf, so as of right now, I'm winning.

Caer, however, won't be so lucky. Scott might be in love with her, he might have spent weeks dreaming about her, but I'd hate to be in her feathers when he realizes that she ripped open the portal with her sword and shoved me into it.

Shove suggests I didn't want to go. Of course I wanted to leave. I'm the one who asked her to do it in the first place. I just didn't expect her to open one so easily, and in Gallean's keep no less. I sorta froze. So yes, she did have to help me along.

Her portal-making ability ought to show Gallean that even though he might be the most powerful wizard, he doesn't know everything about reincarnated gods' powers.

Besides, why shouldn't a physically gifted female, blessed with both beauty and muscle, not be blessed with the ability to create portals and go invisible even in magically denied zones? The gods know I could have used those skills all those years back at Vernal Falls High.

I'm not bitter or anything.

The door to Granda's cottage opens at my arrival. All I had to do was look at it and it swung open for me. It's so nice to be back in a realm where my magic actually works. Like the natural forces of the world appreciate me.

Madigan's jaw drops along with the book he's reading in Scott's favorite chair. "Gigi? What are you doing here?"

"Nice to see you too, Maddie. I can ask you the same."

"Oh, well . . ." he says, lifting the books off his lap and putting them on the table in order to stand up, "I've been staying here since you guys disappeared. Amorin said to make myself at home, so . . ." he gestures to the piles of books sprawled out across the sofa and table, "I did."

"Why aren't you staying with Maria? And what about Alaric? Any news?"

His face blanches. "Declan sent out a decree that anyone searching for Alaric will be excommunicated from the pack."

Excommunicated? That sounds harsh. And suspicious. But I keep those concerns to myself. The best way to get Maddie to talk is to plod along in a happy-go-lucky sort of way and not force anything—not exactly my strong suit. These are the times Scott really comes in handy. Patience isn't really my thing, but I guess since I'm left to my own abilities, I'll try it out.

Get it together, Gigi. You can be calm and collected. You got this.

"Why would he do such a thing?"

There, I did it. I can be positively delightful and polite.

Before Scott and I left for the Shadow Realm, Maddie

would have hung his head in shame, but now, no longer restrained by an alpha or pack position, he holds his chin high. Not cocky or threatening or anything, but secure in himself.

"The alpha role went to his head," he says. "He doesn't want anyone threatening his position, and he definitely doesn't want to lose it to Alaric."

I bet he doesn't, the duplicitous bastard.

"And what does Maria have to say about it?"

His faces pinches as if he swallowed a mouthful of Sour Patch Kids—which I could totally go for, by the way.

Focus, Gigi. Listen to Maddie.

"She's in charge. Declan might be the alpha, but the pack follows whatever she says."

"That still doesn't explain why you're living here."

So much for subtle and smooth. I don't know why I'm reverting to my old disagreeable bitchy self with Maddie. I ought to be relieved that he's been here to keep Granda company and help him and Clarissa. Old habits, I guess.

He smiles at me. "You and Scott welcomed me. You allowed me to reveal all aspects of myself. I've never been able to do that with anyone. I don't feel like a freak with you."

"You are a freak."

His gaze drops to the floor. "I know."

"But so am I, and so is Scott."

A smile erupts on his face. "Thanks."

"Sappy crap aside, where are Granda and Clarissa? I want to know what's been going on the past few days that I've been gone."

"Days? More like weeks."

Weeks? Okay, put a check mark next to "time travel" as a side effect of portal hopping. "Great. Weeks then. So where are they?"

"They're both at the Cathedral. They've been spending all their time there."

"Why aren't they searching for Alaric and Lizzie?"

"There've been some developments."

I do not like the word "developments." It ranks up there with "Fomorian world domination" and "last call."

"What developments?"

He shrugs. "They haven't told me, but ever since you and Scott disappeared from the cavern, they've been a little freaked out."

Understatement of the year.

"Scott and I were a little freaked out too."

His eyes shine with something resemblant of puppy love (and I am well aware of the irony of that). "I didn't know you could make a portal," he says.

"Neither did I."

"And neither did Amorin or Clarissa. You break all the rules."

"Is that what they said?"

His cheeks color with shame. "Yes."

"There's someone in the Shadow Realm who breaks more rules than I do."

He rubs the crystal hanging from his neck and I forget all about goddess rule-breaking, violent acts, and portal ripping. The nightlock-imbued crystal's ability is far more important than anything else right now.

"Did it work? Did it work on the Shadow Moon?"

The largest smile I've ever seen crosses his face. "I didn't shift. Not even a claw came out."

My heart shoots warmth through my body. I might have been harsh to him only a few minutes ago, but Maddie has become part of my family. I may choose aggressive acts over thoughtful word choice more often than not, but I really do want the best for him. "That's amazing."

"You changed my life."

Oh boy. I know I'm a reincarnated goddess and everything, but I really don't like being given credit for "life-changing" experiences. Way too much pressure.

"I didn't."

"Gigi, you did. The crystal stopped the change."

I collapse into Granda's chair. "I wonder how Alaric and Lizzie did at the full moon. It's probably a good thing I wasn't around."

"It's definitely good you weren't, because Declan and Maria's pack are after you."

"There is that . . ."

"I wish I knew how Alaric did, or how he is now. The pack couldn't read each other's minds, but we were together for so many years, it felt like we could. I really miss him."

Memories of the nightmares I had during my time in the Shadow Realm come back to me. The torture Lizzie put Alaric through. The screaming. The moaning. The snarls. What did it all mean?

"Hey, Maddie, could you help me with something?"

He stands at attention, thankful to finally be of use to someone. "What do you need?"

"Grab the candles and matches from the cabinet. We're going to try something."

"Magic?"

Heat begins generating from my fingertips as I pull the Chalice of Healing from its hiding spot behind the false wall by the kitchen.

"Something like that."

Granda's oak table grounds us to the space. After Scott and I fixed it with our powers, no one would be able to tell that it split apart down the middle (or that thick vines shot up through the floor). Oak is a powerful conductor of magic and a grounding element—kinda like the ground wire outside of a house. Since my arrival in Ireland, I've conducted most of my magic outdoors. One, because I wanted to be away from the prying eyes and actions of a father, grandfather, and ancient nun of the Druid Sisters of the Gallicenial. And two, because outdoors I feel at home. I might sleep in a house and spend most of my time indoors, but being outside feels familiar. Whether it be in Vernal Falls, Pennsylvania; Kildare, Ireland; or a Shadow Realm courtyard, the outdoors settles me. But today something tells me I need to conduct this spell indoors. Since I've always tried to listen to the voices in my head (even before the bossy goddess started chatting it up), I go with my gut.

When I conducted tracking spells to find Alaric, I used a map and an article of clothing. My final attempt proved successful. Well, at least it led us to the meeting hall cavern before Scott and I wound up at a wizard's keep via portal. Something needles at my brain that the meeting hall cavern plays an important role in finding Alaric—aside from it being the place he went missing.

This time when I search for Alaric, I need to further ground myself to the space by calling on the Elements. In order to do so, I recall the spell I used when I cast my first circle in Vernal Falls and modify it with some of Scott and Dad's phrases.

"To cast this circle from Earth to Fire, from Water to Air, join together with Spirit to guide me to the answers I seek. I give you my love, my light, as I cast this circle to show me the path to truth. The circle is cast."

Using Scott and Dad's wording brings them into the circle with Maddie and me, or at least their spiritual presence.

"To the East, element of Air, I give to you my love, my light, to show me the path to truth to guard us from sudden storms and protect us with gentle breezes."

The wind, gentle as a butterfly wing, caresses my cheeks, letting me know it came.

"To the South, element of Fire, I give to you my love, my light, to show me the path to truth to guard us from raging fires and warm us with controlled flames."

The candles' flames shoot into the air. My feet and palms crackle with heat, albeit controlled.

"To the West, element of Earth, I give to you my love, my light, to show me the path to truth to guard us from disturbance by providing firm footing."

The feeling of blanket covers my entire body, weighing me to the ground as the scent of fresh soil fills the air.

To the North, element of Water, I give to you my love, my light, to show me the path to truth to guard us from tidal waves and cradle us in calm waters as gentle as a mother's arms."

My body feels as if its floating in a warm pool of water, cocooned against the cold.

"I call to the Elements for guidance in my search. I offer the Chalice of Healing, not as a permanent token, but as an inspiration to spur ideas. My blood, however," I raise a knife from the table to my palm, "is my token of gratitude for your presence tonight. Take the blood of a goddess as payment for the help I will be calling upon you for this evening."

Maddie leans over the table to whisper to me as if the Elements might overhear us talking and he wants to keep his question a secret. What he doesn't realize is that they can hear him without him even vocalizing it. I might be a mind reader, but the Elements go beyond even my ability.

"What are you going to ask them to do?"

"Find Alaric, of course."

His eyes widen. The gold halos around his pupils remind

me of Alaric's. I wonder if it's a werewolf thing (I don't know enough of them personally to form an opinion on the matter) or perhaps a good person thing, or one heck of a coincidence —though in my recent experiences that line of thinking is naive. Universal alignments abound in all aspects of life.

I close my eyes and focus on what visions the Elements might offer me.

I see a rolling countryside—not helpful or specific. An underground prison—more helpful but still not specific. A flash of Alaric strapped to a table—just like my nightmares. Soon a flash of him walking around in the underground prison, but it no longer seems likes he's a prisoner. He can come and go as he pleases. I don't want to think too hard on the reasons why he hasn't left yet. I also fight the temptation to open my eyes and take off searching for him, because I still don't know his exact location. Apparently one can summon patience during times of duress.

He's somewhere vaguely familiar to me. I concentrate on where he is. I imagine myself walking down a circular staircase with stone steps. I descend deeper and deeper until I reach a narrow stone corridor.

"What do you see?" Maddie whispers.

"The hallway has doorways to different chambers."

"Can you tell which one Alaric is in?"

I pull my lips in, concentrating on my surroundings. The feel of flesh further grounds me to my vision space. I enter a doorway on my right. It's a room gilded with gold. There are intricately woven tapestries of bucolic scenes hanging from the walls. There's even a gold statue off in the corner near an altar. I study the sculpture for a long time, not understanding what my vision is revealing to me.

"What is it?" Maddie whispers.

"There's a large gold statue in the room."

"Who is it of?"

My gaze falls to the long wavy hair and the full breasts. "A woman."

"A goddess?"

"Of . . . someone's coming."

I hide beside the statue. Habit, I guess. In my vision state, I don't think anyone can see or hear me—at least I hope to the gods they can't—but still, it's better to be safe than make an irreparable mistake. The gods know I've already had enough experience doing that.

Alaric walks into the room and stops before the statue. He's just as handsome as I remember with his chiseled jaw, strong muscles, and an all-consuming sense of power.

"I used to love you," he says. His voice sounds like he drank battery acid.

"But now?" I whisper, hoping, fearing, he can hear me.

In answer, he slashes out at the statue and gashes it with claws that have shot out of his fingers. The scrap of claw against metal sends shivers down my spine—worse than fingers on a chalkboard and far more heartbreaking.

"Well done, my son, well done," someone says from the doorway.

I peek around the statue, unable to believe who I'm hearing.

"He's supposed to be sealed away," I whimper. "He's supposed to be immured." I take in the gold statue, the tapestries. I've been here before.

Maddie grips my arms, pulling me back from my vision state, back from Brigit's shrine room. "Who is? Alaric?"

Tears run down my cheeks. "No, Clayone."

2

HIGH PRIESTESS

*C*aer thought she knew who she was. After her shift into the swan and back again, she felt secure in her identity, but after ripping a portal for Gigi, and after Scott's reaction, she was not so sure. When Scott wasn't ignoring her, he cast glares at her more lethal than a thousand knife stabs. She savored the training Gallean provided them. It was not only a distraction but also assured her that she was following the correct path—that pushing Gigi through the portal hadn't been a terrible idea. It was an act predetermined by the Fates, and Caer was their instrument.

Providing Gigi with the means to depart had allowed Gallean to renew Caer's training. Her practice battles with Scott pushed her to master not only her skill but her ability to interact with the man who managed to leave her breathless—and not because of the physical exertion of sparring with him. Sometimes she regretted not having run a sword through his throat when she'd had the chance. That way she wouldn't be distracted during her training. Love weakened the mighty.

"Again," Gallean shouted, bringing her back to the

present. "You must always be in the moment when you're fighting. You cannot disappear into your own head or a portal."

She met his sword with her own. "But I can create a portal at will."

"That may be, but it comes at a cost."

The wizard had jarred her. "What cost?"

"For every natural rule you break, there comes a consequence."

How could a god, even a reincarnated one, break a natural rule? And if she could, why was it in violation? What cost was Gallean referring to?

"Gigi is in danger, isn't she." Scott pointed at Caer. "She put her at risk by sending her through the portal while in your keep, and now, Gigi will suffer." His lip curled as he squinted at her.

Sadness replaced any longing she once felt in his presence. If her portal caused Gigi harm, the gap between her and Scott would become too expansive to bridge. Again she regretted not running him through.

"Enough, Scott. Caer gave Gigi what she wanted. Your sister was intent on leaving, and you are well aware that when she sets her mind to do something, she will achieve it."

Gallean tried to justify Caer's actions as if she was still a young princess and incapable of making her own rational decisions. But she didn't need his protection. Not now. Not ever. She had needed him when Balor and his men set out to find her, killing Mathair Mhór and Nimblefoot in the process. She had needed him when she was starving and weak, surviving only because of the berries she found outside the cave. She had needed him to choose her when Scott and Gigi arrived early. She did not need his protection now.

She angled her sword at Scott in challenge. "Then fight

me. Show me that you can stand alongside me in battle and not falter at the sight of Balor and his men."

Scott pulled his sword from his scabbard and angled it at her.

Gallean rested his head on his folded hands. "Intense emotion can serve as a powerful ally while on the battlefield."

"Exactly," Scott and Caer murmured together.

"But, it will leave you weak after a battle."

"Not if you win," Scott growled through gritted teeth.

"Do not count on victory," Caer hissed.

"You must ensure another enemy is not waiting for the opportunity to run a knife through you before you recover."

Scott swung his sword in a high-arcing, exaggerated motion. "I'm not worried."

Caer mimicked his action. He would not best her in swordplay. The sword and she were allies. "Nor am I."

"So both of you are prepared to take me on when this battle is finished?"

Caer and Scott faltered.

Gallean latched on to the surprise. "Yes, if you dare fight in anger, I will take on the winner, and I can assure you that neither of you are ready for that challenge."

Again the wizard injected himself into her life as if he were a great protector, an indulgent uncle of sorts. Hunger and cold were not desired treats for anyone.

"You. Do. Not. Know. What. I. Am. Capable. Of," Caer ground out.

Scott glared at her. "Neither do you."

"Enough. Both of you." Gallean quickly lifted his hands into the air and flung them outward. A burst of energy knocked them both to the ground. "I will not have the two of you at each other's throats. Your enemies reside beyond these walls. This bickering halts your true purpose and hinders your training."

Scott slowly pushed himself off the ground. Not to be bested, Caer leapt up before he was back on his feet.

He rolled his eyes at her. "At times you act so much like Gigi, it is uncanny."

Unwilling to relinquish her anger, she said through clenched jaw, "I will take that as a compliment."

Scott slipped his sword back into his scabbard before shaking his head. "Oh gods, you even talk like her."

Not letting herself be distracted by Scott's softening attitude toward her, she shoved her sword into its scabbard for dramatic effect before folding her arms behind her back. "My true purpose is to kill Balor. Is it not?"

"Your true purpose is to join with Scott and Gigi in their protection of the human race."

"Whoa," Scott said, stepping in front of her as if to protect her from Gallean. "Saving the entire human race seems awfully drastic. I was under the impression we just kill the one-eyed Fomorian giant, take out a few of his men, then Caer's thirst for revenge will be sated, and we can rejoin Gigi and end the Fomorian takeover."

Gallean took an iron poker and pushed the ash around in the fire pit. As the coals turned red hot, he threw a few dry logs on the fire. Soon flames appeared. It was apparent that the wizard was withholding information from them.

"Tell us, Gallean, what else is there to know?" Scott walked over to the now-blazing fire.

"There are many pieces to the puzzle."

Caer remembered the puzzles from her childhood that her nursemaid always tried to get her to play with. She did not like them then. She most definitely did not like them now.

"I am not interested in games."

"Think of it as many different strands of jute pulled and

twisted to eventually form a thick rope that a single cut from the sharpest blade cannot slice."

Caer stepped toward them. "And who is weaving this rope?"

"That is what we do not know."

Scott paced in front of the fire. The heat of the flames was unable to warm either side of his body because he was moving at Otherworldly godly speed. But really, who could blame him? Gallean had dropped a freaking bomb on them, and he was still in shock. For the hundredth time since Gigi disappeared through the portal, he wished she were here. She'd know what to say. Not necessarily what to do, but she'd drop a stream of curses on Gallean that would at least give Scott some time to think over everything, to be the one capable of acting rationally in the face of incomprehensible information.

Caer had been no help whatsoever. She hadn't said a freaking word since Gallean's announcement. Scott didn't think she had even moved. A gorgeous marble statue. She had to be in shock, and that wasn't going to help any of them. And if he freaked out and went all explosive Oegden power, Caer and Gallean would be on the receiving end of a Scott-sized tornado. He didn't think the keep could handle that terrible force. He needed to pull himself together to figure this shit out. He took a deep breath, a trick he'd learned from watching Gigi, and began to slow down so that at least he was moving at regular human speed.

"Let me get this straight," he said, finally moving slowly enough to feel the heat from the fire. "We've got Balor and his Fomorian cronies plus Maria, who might be Carman, and her werewolf squad. Who else is there?"

Caer shifted to face him, finally snapping out of her frozen shock. Scott swallowed the lump in his throat. She took his breath away in the most clichéd way imaginable. Memories of their kiss still teased his brain (and other parts of him), but there wasn't time for a romantic interlude, especially when he was still pissed off at her for shoving Gigi through the portal.

"Who is this Carman and her werewolf squad?"

Gods, even her deep, throaty voice was sexy. But again, time to focus.

"An ancient witch who may have possessed a girl and taken control of a local werewolf pack ever since their leader, Alaric, went missing."

"Is she responsible for the leader's disappearance?"

Scott stopped pacing. He had never thought about that. He'd been so focused on helping Gigi find Alaric that he'd never considered that Carman could be stowing him away for safekeeping for some twisted diabolical plan. Gigi assumed it was Breas, her scorned ex-boyfriend-slash-god-slash-Otherworldly estranged husband, but maybe it was Carman.

"Carman helped raise Alaric. She would have access to him no matter what her form. Gigi blamed Breas for kidnapping Alaric."

"Breas?" she said, turning the name over in her mouth. "That name is familiar to me. Why?"

Scott only remembered flashes of Oegden's life. He suspected Caer had some from her goddess life too.

"Breas is an actual god returned from the Otherworld, and therefore immortal."

Caer cracked her neck. It was an impressive display of might. "Gallean, can he be killed?"

Gallean continued working the fire. "Anyone can be killed."

If Gigi were here, she'd tell Gallean that he was helpful as always, but Scott didn't want to be quite so sarcastic. Gigi wasn't often able to elicit responses with her strategy. She relied on Scott for that skill set. He called upon it now.

"Is that something we should do?"

"Perhaps," Gallean replied.

Caer glared at the wizard. She really did resemble his sister in certain aspects of her personality. Especially Gigi's lack of patience.

"Do I need to kill him too?"

Gallean pointed at her. "That is not your purpose."

She threw back her head and growled. "I'm tired of people telling me what my purpose is and what I can and can't do."

Gods, her growls were sexy too. He wondered what sort of sounds she'd make if he trailed kisses down her throat.

Scott, focus.

Gallean added another log to the fire. To an outsider, it would seem that he was disinterested in their conversation, but after spending time with him, Scott knew he was instructing in his own way.

"Discovery of one's purpose will guide each of you in your journey."

She whipped her body around to face him. "And how are we to discover this purpose?"

"By training and focus."

Scott slumped down into the seat beside Gallean. "How did I know you were going to say that?"

"Because, at times, you are very wise."

Wisdom seemed like an admirable trait, but Scott suspected that Gallean was holding back everything he wanted to say.

"And at other times?"

"You are impulsive and easily manipulated."

"Ouch. Go right for the jugular, why don't you. I wouldn't say I'm impulsive or easily manipulated."

"When it comes to your sister you are. She can talk you into anything."

Scott would never admit that fact to Gigi or anyone else, but Gallean spoke the truth. When it came to his sister, he was willing to do anything, including form questionable alliances and engage in his own treacherous manipulation if required. To be blunt, he would do anything to get her back.

He glanced over at Caer, who was too busy studying the flames to notice him. Maybe he could convince her to rip open another portal. Gigi needed his help. The longer they were separated from each other, the more he worried about her. She possessed an innate talent for getting in trouble, but aside from that, it was his job as her human brother as well as her immortal one to save her. He would not fail Gigi the way Caer had failed him.

Caer shyly peeked at him, as if reading his mind, but Scott didn't think that was one of her gifts. He would use her affection toward him to his advantage. He cared about her. In the Otherworld she was—is, he supposed—his true love, but in this form, his sole purpose was to protect Gigi, and he would do whatever he needed to in order to accomplish that goal. No matter who he used. No matter who he left behind.

"There are always consequences," Gallean murmured.

Consequences were the least of Scott's concern.

3

WEREWOLF REVIVAL

*W*TF. Clayone is supposed to be immured. I locked him in Brigit's shrine myself. Well, with the help of the cows, but still, he was locked away.

Exactly. Locked away. Not dead, Brigit says.

"Did you know he could have outside contact?"

I suspected as much.

"Does your throat burn when you lie? Because you should feel like you drank battery acid. Alaric's voice sure sounded like he did."

Very well. I knew he wasn't dead, but so did you.

"I thought he'd desiccate and die."

With all your magical experiences leading up to Samhain and in the days following, were you not told you are unable to permanently maim another living thing?

"Oh."

Yes, oh. You imprisoned him, but you did not kill him.

"I assumed that the rules of my magic wouldn't apply to Clayone."

You assumed incorrectly.

"But he's permanently imprisoned. I did do that."

Maddie gently squeezes my arms. "Who are you talking to?"

My eyes shift back into the present. "I was talking out loud, wasn't I."

"Yes, but I only heard one side of the conversation. Who was it?"

There's no point lying to him. Besides, I don't want my throat to burn. Since I arrived in Ireland, I've pretty much stopped lying, and the lining of my esophagus is all healed. I'd rather not start again. I'm out of practice, and my throat tolerance is gone.

"Brigit."

He drops his hands as his eyes widen. "The goddess? You speak to the goddess?" The wonder in his eyes makes me uncomfortable. He knows I'm the goddess reincarnated, but the way he's looking at me goes beyond rock star status.

"Sometimes."

"Is Clayone alive?"

"You know his name?"

"I'm a werewolf. I've heard the legends."

Maddie always seems to know so much more than he lets on. I don't think he willingly withholds information from me. He just doesn't realize how vital everything he knows is. I always have to draw it out of him, leading question after leading question.

"Did you know Clayone is Alaric's dad?"

His hands follow the knots on Granda's table. I could draw every single knot on Gram's oak table from memory. Granda's is fast becoming familiar too.

But the cottage air is too dense for me. I need fresh air to clear my mind so I can think. I get up and start walking outside.

Maddie follows me. "Alaric never talked about his dad. I only knew that his father wasn't around. But then, none of the pack spoke about their parents. I don't know if anyone actually even had parents they could keep in touch with. Most of us were created the same way."

We've never discussed how he or the rest of the pack were created. Gods know I read all sorts of werewolf creation methods from Carman's book, and I saw the jail cells in the cavern from the scores of werewolf failures that occurred before she found an effective means to procreate them.

"Who sired you, Madigan?"

"Alaric bit me. I turned at the next full moon."

All those times Alaric's mouth had traced along the lines of my throat.

"He bit you? That's awful."

"It wasn't so bad. We were young. He didn't want to bite me. Somehow Carman made him do it. I don't think he even remembers doing it. He was spelled or something."

That theory would line up with Alaric's midnight visit to my room and why he hadn't known how he got there. He was really upset. He told me about other times that he had done things he wasn't proud of—things he didn't remember. He even mentioned blood on his hands.

I swallow, trying hard not to think of other things Alaric might have done when he wasn't in control of himself. "Who sired the rest of the pack?"

He shrugs. "Alaric, I guess."

After what I saw in my vision with Alaric's fingers transforming into claws without the aid of the moon, I am shit-ass scared. I walk over to Maddie and squeeze his arms. "Are you able to shift outside of the full moon?"

He tries to pull away, but I squeeze tighter, my nails biting into his skin.

"No, no, we can only turn at the full moon."

Touching him, I get a full read on him. He holds on to that belief with all his being.

I focus all my energy, all my magic on him, forcing him to either reveal it verbally or physically. I squeeze with everything I have. "Tell me the truth, Madigan. Can you turn?"

Wolf eyes flash before me. Claws protrude from his fingernails. Sharp canines elongate from his teeth.

He breaks away from me, halfway shifted into the wolf he was created to be. "What's happening to me? I'm wearing the crystal."

I reveal the crystal hanging from my wrist. "No, you're not."

I hold it up for him, and he swipes it back with his claws and shifts back to himself.

"How did that happen? I'm only supposed to be able to turn at the full moon. What did you do to me?" Fear seeps from every pore of his body.

"I suspect that Clayone and Carman found a loophole to the curse."

"What's the loophole?"

"Not what. Who."

His body stiffens. He immediately realizes who I'm referring to. "But Alaric was never able to turn outside of the full moon either."

"Do you know that for certain?"

He studies the ground in front of him. "No."

"And that is why we should join forces," Breas says, appearing before us as if out of thin air.

My first impulse is to try to punch him, but he's ready for it and knocks my hand to the side as if it's nothing more than a minor inconvenience.

"As I told you back in Vernal Falls, you're so very

predictable. It made catching you so simple. I didn't even need to use my backup plan."

I lunge at him. I might not be able to shift my fingernails into wolf claws, but they can certainly exact damage.

He rolls his eyes and snaps his fingers. Someone wraps their arms around me from behind, pinning me in place.

I kick. I claw. I fight to break free, but my captive has me in their clutches.

Maddie shouts, "Hey!" but that's all he says before his body hits the ground. I jerk around and see him bound with rope and gagged.

Breas waves his finger in front of my face. I wish I could bite it off, but he's just out of biting range.

"Tsk, tsk, tsk. Gigi, I expected better from you."

I hiss through clenched teeth. "You kidnapped Alaric and Lizzie. You stinking bastard. I ought to—"

"Ryan, if you would."

An arm shifts from my waist, and a hand claps to my mouth before I can take advantage of the "freedom." Then Breas's words reach my brain.

Ryan . . .

I try a ninja move that always works in the movies. A drop-twirl-kick-punch. Trouble is, it's not working for me. But I need to break free. I need to see who this Ryan is.

Could it be Ryan? Our Ryan?

But our Ryan is dead. I saw him die. I heard the gunshot. I felt his claws swipe at the back of my legs in a last-ditch effort to kill me. I watched Lizzie's spirit form come for him, and I watched his spirit leave his body to be with her. It was beautiful. It was magnificent. Could it have been a lie?

I keep spinning, twirling, punching, but nothing is working. If it really is our Ryan holding me, I wouldn't be able to break free. His freakishly strong hands never dropped a pigskin—they certainly aren't going to drop me. I have so many questions racing through my brain, but fighting prevents me from asking them. I focus on Breas's mind, a slimy slick place I really don't want to be in, but it serves a purpose. I drop a single word. *Please.*

He shifts his feet. He tosses his shoulders around. He keeps looking at me then looking away. I recognize his movements for what they are. A god struggling with indecision and—what is that? A conscience?

Breas cares about me, albeit in his twisted way. He's afraid I'll ruin all his plans.

I file that factoid away for safekeeping. I'll use it in the future. Maybe not at the first opportunity—that would be too impulsive, too reincarnated Gigi—but maybe when the situation really is life or death. That's when I'll take advantage of his feelings for me.

Finally, he crosses his arms and says, "Fine. Ryan, let her talk."

I turn my head enough to see Ryan's profile. After weeks sitting side by side at the principal's office back in Vernal Falls, I'd know his forehead, his nose, and his lips anywhere. I let out a relief sob. Everything is going to be okay.

"How are you alive?"

Ryan doesn't reply. He doesn't say or do anything.

I try to get a read on him, but he's blocked off to me.

"Your little goddess tricks won't work on him. He's under my control."

Breas reasserts his power, pushing all indecision and any mind access away. Now I can only plead with him in the hopes that his feelings for me remain useful.

"I watched him get shot. I watched his spirit leave."

"Ha!" Breas doubles over laughing.

I fling my fists to hit him, but Ryan keeps me in his stronghold. All I can do is watch Breas with his freaking head bent over as he slaps the tops of his thighs in hysterics.

When he's had his fun, he stands back up with a wicked grin across his face. "You mean with the silver bullet in the antique silver gun?"

And there it is. The truth in all its spit-in-your-face reality.

"You knew about it."

"Of course I knew about it. Rose never locked her doors, at least not before you released Clayone—brilliant job by the way. Remember the night I got you drunk on Irish whiskey? Which you thought was a cliché? Really it was just the simplest means to get you to forget your loathing of me."

My stomach turns over. I remember the night. Well, most of it. Along with the neck full of hickeys the next day.

"Even when you were wasted on whiskey, you still refused to have sex with me, holding on to your hate of me like the most intimate of lovers. Like the lovers we used to be," he says, his lighthearted mocking turning dark and angry.

I glare at him. I hate him now more than ever.

"I switched the bullets in the gun that night." He circles around me. "I couldn't have my . . . little experiment getting killed. I needed allies on this side to assist me."

"You call bobblehead Kensey an ally?"

He drags a finger across the line of my jaw. "Oh, Gigi, jealousy becomes you."

At one time the gesture might have brought me to my knees. I might have even blacked out. But not today. Today I want to break every bone in his finger along with the rest of him.

I will not leave room for doubt.

"I. Am. Not. Jealous."

"Whatever you say, love," he says. "Kensey served other purposes. She addressed my carnal needs well—a role I asked you to fill, by the way."

My lip snarls at him on its own. My entire body loathes him completely.

"Her attractiveness also allowed her to venture into places I couldn't go." He shakes his head, smiling at me. "Your boyfriend's old pack really doesn't like you."

I will not let him get to me. I will not.

"Tell me something I don't already know."

"Very well. Ryan was an unintended gift from Clayone."

"How do you mean?"

"Do you remember that Sunday evening when you were still recovering from your Friday night exploits?"

"And my Saturday night mistakes."

He narrows his eyes. "Saturday night you wanted me. I called for you and you came. My, how you came."

Biles creeps up my throat. I force it down. He will not win. I will break him with my words.

"Must not have been that great since I don't even remember."

His jaw feathers with tension.

Good job, Gi. The bitch still rules!

"Regardless, the little camping trip Ryan suggested?"

That was Lizzie's idea, or at least that's what Ryan told me . . .

Give him nothing, Gi. Give him nothing.

"Yes," I reply without any emotion.

"Who do you think gave him that idea?"

Tiny fissures eat at my cool, expressionless facade.

Keep it together, Gi. Keep it together.

"Why?"

He shakes his head. "I'm not divulging all my secrets to you as if we're lovers. Oh wait, we were. But you've learned more than enough for now."

He snaps his fingers. "Ryan?"

Ryan lifts me up to carry me. I struggle to break out of his grip, but it's useless. He's like the freaking Incredible Hulk.

"Where are you taking me?"

Breas waggles his finger at me. "No, no. I will not be voicing that juicy morsel. There are far too many supernatural beings with powerful hearing."

Speaking of supernatural beings, Maddie hasn't moved since he fell. Wisps of smoke swirl in the air above his wrists. Wolfsbane.

"What are you going to do with him? You can't just leave him with the wolfsbane rope. He'll die."

Breas rubs his face and laughs. "I forgot how entertaining your Earthly form is. Of course I'm going to leave him."

"But—"

Breas snaps his fingers again. Ryan wraps his arm across my mouth. I should bite him, but it's Ryan. My friend who always defended my honor. Who stood by my side when I needed him. Who remained my friend even when he became an iconic star on the high school football team.

My friend who I thought was dead and is now a werewolf working for Breas.

Who is magicked to work for Breas.

Nice of you to show up. I thought Breas didn't possess magic.

He has some. His ability to compel is strong enough at times to affect even you, but his magic is nowhere near as powerful as yours or Scott's.

Carman?

They are no longer aligned.

Then who is Breas working with?

Not who. What.

Oh gods, what?

Silence.

My gods, sometimes they really freaking pissed me off. Just when you think you've met all the nasties in the world, you find one from another one.

4

ACE OF SWORDS

*H*olding on to her belief that Scott would come around, Caer left him to his ramblings about who could be weaving the thick rope. She suspected it was Balor, but then, although the giant was evil and lethal to anyone he cast his eye upon, she doubted he was capable of intricate, vengeful plans beyond that which he could see. Her memories of him were of a monster, a hideous one-eyed giant pirate, not someone capable of manipulating multiple complicated plots behind the scenes. And with his ability to turn to stone anyone he set his eye upon, he would not need to be a master planner of intricate plots.

In her room she paced back and forth, using the contours of the rug as her center. Scott confused her above anything else.

Killing Balor might pose challenges she may not be completely prepared for, but interacting with Scott beyond fighting was far beyond her comfort zone. When she had first arrived through the window and kissed him, she'd been brave. But she hadn't taken the time to consider the consequences of kissing him beyond the moment when their lips touched, including how they'd interact with each other following the kiss. She also hadn't planned on ripping open a portal for Gigi, but Gigi's overwhelming and singular desire to go home spoke to Caer in a way she couldn't resist.

Scott had mentioned that Caer and Gigi were alike several times. She suspected that was the real reason she opened the portal for Gigi. She could give Gigi what she wanted. Everything Caer desired was at Gallean's, aside from killing Balor. But she wasn't ready to fight him on her own. She needed more training and lessons in battle strategy.

And, as much as she hated relying on anyone, she needed Scott.

She didn't know what that said about her. After spending most of her life on her own, why did she need a man to help her?

She remembered back to the day Mathair Mhór pulled the Lovers card.

"Your true love has returned to life on another plane. There he serves as a protector. The duality of his life will come to a crossroads. When he stands at the pinnacle of understanding himself, his power, and his true purpose, he will go on a quest."

Caer had latched on to the idea of a quest, and when she asked Mathair Mhór what sort of quest, the old woman told Caer he would go in search of her and would fight for her.

Caer had lashed out with her sword at the prospect that a man would fight for her. She hated the notion that she couldn't protect herself. It was the true reason she left the cottage that day in a fit of rage and fell asleep on the fated mountain when Mathair Mhór and Nimblefoot perished in the fire.

What would have happened if she hadn't run away? Would she have died too, or would she have been taken prisoner? And if they took her prisoner, would Mathair Mhór and Nimblefoot have been allowed to live?

She had never let her mind entertain that thought before, but now it ate away at her, threatening to shift her attention away from her current situation. She shook her body to rid it of the growing regret. Regret didn't solve problems. Action did.

Mathair Mhór's words, *"He will fight for you . . ."* echoed in her mind.

From what she could gather from overheard conversations, Scott was the reincarnated god Oegden, which would explain his speed and strength.

When she was at Lake of the Dragon Mouth, the lake bordering her father's castle, she figured out she was the reincarnated goddess Caer Ibormeith. According to the legends, Oegden was the goddess's counterpart. But, in human form, Scott was a mortal man capable of disappointment and failure.

Weak.

Breakable.

Breathtakingly handsome.

She grabbed a book and sat down on the bed. She would not daydream about Scott's good looks nor their kiss. Neither one would help her cause.

She soon fell into the story of two young women who were tasked with delivering a scroll to an old woman referred to as Mathair Mhór—could it be the same woman who had raised her? She recognized the name of the great warrior of legend, Cu Chulainn, who Mathair Mhór had raised long before Caer arrived, but she didn't know when. She never thought to ask Mathair Mhór how old she was. Now she would never know. Mathair Mhór's story was over. Caer added to her growing pile of regret but refused to dwell on it.

She immediately liked the boy who assisted Ris with the

injured capall. Acts of kindness, no matter how small, always brought a smile to her lips and warmed her heart.

A knock tore her away from the tale. Caer's heart pounded rapidly. Could it be Gallean come to kick her out? The wizard had been immensely upset with her at first for ripping open the portal and pushing Gigi through it, but he had quickly forgiven her and had told them that Gigi had completed her training. But maybe now he had changed his mind and was angry that Caer had broken apart the trí cumhacht, or that she was able to conduct magic in his keep when he could not, or for some other reason that as of yet she could not fathom.

Or perhaps it was Scott coming to apologize for his earlier behavior? The possibility made her want to run to the door and throw it open. But too much enthusiasm on her part would demonstrate the power Scott held over her, and she would not bow to any man. Restraint would serve her well.

"You may enter," she called out.

Scott walked into the room. Her stomach did that backflip thing it tended to do whenever she saw him. She swallowed the saliva forming in her mouth. It also would not do to let on that he made her nervous.

Scott toyed with a glass object on a shelf. "Where did you grow up? You sound so formal."

"I grew up in a castle with servants. My nursemaid insisted I speak this way."

He pulled over a chair and made himself comfortable. "A castle? Were you a princess?"

There was no point denying her childhood. Scott knew about Balor, but nothing else. The two lived a lifetime apart. They were strangers.

"I was, but I did not dream of being saved by a faraway prince."

He laughed. "Of course you didn't. You're much too stubborn to ever acknowledge you need help."

Caer wasn't sure if that was a compliment or an attack on her character. She decided to leave it alone for the present. However, she planned to discuss that point later.

"So your parents were a king and queen?"

"My mother died in childbirth. I never knew her."

His eyes grew watery. "I'm sorry. I shouldn't have brought it up."

He struck her as overly sensitive. It was an emotion she never truly allowed herself to feel. Denial gave one strength.

She closed the book. "No matter. A person cannot mourn for someone she did not know."

He leaned toward her. "Sure you can. I didn't remember my mom because she died when I was two, but I still missed her. I still longed for her, but then . . ."

His story intrigued her. He talked with such heartfelt emotion that he lulled her in, and now that he had stopped, a part of her considered punching him in the stomach to keep going.

Far too much time passed, or she was impatient—probably both—but he couldn't just sit there after drawing her into his own tale.

"But then what?"

He cleared his throat. "But then, I shot my friend."

She stiffened. "Shot? What is shot?"

He released a sigh. "My best friend, Ryan, was turning into a werewolf. At the beginning of October on the night of the first full moon of the month, he tried to kill Gigi. I took a gun," she stared blankly at him, "basically it's a metal rod that can shoot a fireball, but instead of fire or magic it's made of metal, in this case silver."

"Why?"

He smothered his face with his hands. "Silver is one of the only ways to kill a werewolf."

"And a werewolf is a human who can turn into a wolf."

"Yes."

"And your friend turned into a werewolf and wanted to kill your sister."

He pulled in his lips and nodded.

"Why?"

"Because Gigi is the Goddess Brigit reincarnated."

"But how did your friend become a werewolf? Was he born that way?"

"No, he was bitten by the Original Werewolf, Clayone."

That name sounded familiar to her.

"Clayone, you say?"

She opened the book on her lap, flipped through a few pages, and handed it to him. "Spelled like this?" She pointed to the name.

"Yes, where did you find this?" he asked as he closed it to look at the cover. *The Druid Sisters of the Gallicenial?*

"From one of the bookshelves."

He skimmed through a few pages before looking over at her. That sparkle that always made her nervous returned to his eyes. "This story is about Clarissa, Carman, and Clayone."

"It's about a young boy named Niall as well," Gallean said from the open doorway.

"Never heard of him," Scott said, returning to the story.

The great wizard walked into the room and stood before them. "No, I don't suppose you have. Niall's spirit left his body. The assumption is that he died."

Scott threw up his hands. "Spoiler alert!"

He certainly was dramatic at times. Caer prided herself on being grounded. Practical. And far less loud.

"What happened to him?" she asked.

"His spirit was brought back and tied to another. But

together, after a time, their magic became too powerful. Rather than cause rifts in the Earthly Realm, he found an island not conducive to the conduction of magic."

"And that's why you can shift into a bear."

"I left behind my forename, Niall, and adopted Gallean. You are a bright woman."

"And what am I?" Scott asked. The uncertainty in his voice now did not match the personality she had come to enjoy in their short time together.

"You will find reserves of strength you did not know you possess, for you readily embrace what Caer and Gigi fear."

"And what is that?"

Gallean smiled. "That is for you to figure out. It is time for this old man to go to bed," he said and left the room without any further explanation.

Scott remained seated, wringing his hands.

Caer couldn't understand why Scott was so uncomfortable. She didn't have much experience with talking to people about their deepest dreams and regrets, but she figured if she had learned how to hammer-fist a man's throat at twelve, she could very well learn how to talk to someone. Even if it was someone who made her heart race.

"What is bothering you?" she asked, much quieter than she intended. Her question felt far more intimate than it was meant to.

"I'm worried about my sister," he whispered.

She already knew that. It was what he wasn't saying that she wanted to know. "But . . ."

He released a long sigh. "But I don't know if I'm capable of what has been foreseen for me. The reserves of strength and the ability to end lives."

There were many years when Caer had lived on her own that she feared the monsters that walked the earth. It kept her up at night and drove her during the day. Her arm muscles bulged as she tightened them to prove to herself that she was strong and dangerous. That the monsters should fear her.

"I will do it for you."

He smiled at her. Her knees felt weak. She was glad she wasn't standing. Why could a harmless smile, one Scott gave freely to anyone he encountered, weaken her so?

"That I don't doubt, but I won't have you killing for me."

She lifted her chin. He walked on dangerous ground with that statement. "Because I am a woman?"

"Oh gods, no. Believe me, I have no problem with fierce females prowling around and kicking ass. If I did, Gigi would have adjusted my attitude a long time ago."

She envied the way he spoke about his sister with so much love and appreciation. Gigi was never far from his mind. Caer wondered if someday she'd find a place there too.

"What is it then?"

He dragged his hands along his legs. "Life is precious. It's a gift. And even if someone doesn't treat other living things that way, it doesn't mean their own lifeblood should be ended."

"So the man who tried to take advantage of me even after I told him to stop deserved to live?"

He shot up from his seat. "What?"

"After you and Gigi arrived, Gallean told me not to return. I went to the village to find—" Caer paused. She went there to find satisfaction. To be kissed and caressed by someone other than the one she wanted the most. The one sitting next to her now. The one still furious at her for ripping open a portal for his sister.

Should she tell him the truth or lie? She had always told the truth. She'd never had a reason to lie. In truth, she'd never had anyone to lie to. But with Scott standing before her, she could not risk any further rejection from him.

"To get money to buy my way off the island."

He furrowed his eyebrows at her. "To get money?"

"Yes, that's how you leave a place, is it not?"

A dimple popped out on his cheek. His eyes took on a dangerous glint. "It is, but not when you can create portals. What was the true reason, Caer?"

The way he said her name made her squeamish. That need for satisfaction returned, but this time, the cause was standing in front of her.

"To find . . ." she began, and he stepped toward her.

"Yes . . ."

She swallowed hard. His proximity was making it more difficult to lie.

"To find . . ."

He dropped to his knees in front of her. He was tall enough that even on his knees they were almost eye to eye. "Caer, what were you trying to find?"

A sharp ache pulsed between her legs. She refused to tell him what she really wanted, but she could not continue lying. He didn't believe her anyway.

"I tried to find you."

He stood up and backed away from her. "Thank you."

She could breathe easier now that he wasn't so close, but she missed his warmth. "For what?"

He licked his lips. "For admitting that you wanted me."

He had skillfully backed her into a symbolic corner, but that wouldn't stop her from fighting. "I did not say I wanted you. Just that I wanted to find you."

He approached her with purpose. She sucked in a breath. He reached for her white tuft of hair and pushed it behind her ear. She closed her eyes in anticipation of what was coming next and waited.

And waited.

Finally, she opened them to an empty room.

5

CHAINED AND BOUND

*R*yan winds a chain around my body multiple times while Breas watches with a stupid grin that I want to knock right off his face. But it's Ryan I'm really concerned about. I keep trying to get him to look at me, but he refuses to meet my gaze. His eyes are black orbs—Breas took full possession of him. But how? Brigit said he can compel, but this blank gaze goes far beyond that. It must be whatever he has under his command.

But Breas won't win. Not if I can help it.

I struggle against the chains in an effort to get Ryan's attention, but I can't move. The freaking chains are too tight.

He continues to ignore me anyway.

I focus all my attention on him. His mind's blocked off to me, but I try to drop a single thought into his. *Are these silver?*

He keeps pulling the chain in and around my legs so tight the links will leave permanent impressions on my skin.

"Are these silver?" I whisper low and quiet enough for only a werewolf to hear me.

Still he ignores me.

"Are these silver?" I say louder, no longer caring if Breas

overhears and hoping beyond hope that the third time really is the charm.

"He won't speak to you. He's been compelled not to interact with you in any way. But, yes, the chains are silver," Breas says from his perch in the far corner of this . . . cell. A freaking jail cell.

As much as I'd like to figure out where the hell I am, I'll worry about my location when I'm alone. For now I need to find out everything I can about Ryan.

"How can he handle them without getting burned?"

Breas laughs, reminding me of fingernails on a chalkboard. My body swells with tension.

"Ryan, show the prisoner your hands."

Ryan lifts his palms, revealing severe burns.

"You monster," I whimper. "Why are you doing this to him?"

Breas stalks over to me. "I remember your little vine trick from the last time you were imprisoned. Silver chains suppress magic."

"But why are you making Ryan suffer for it?"

He drags a finger along my jaw. His touch makes me want to vomit all over his black leather pants. I mean, honestly, black leather? I hope he sweats profusely, drops them to use the bathroom, then can't get them back up. With his pants halfway up his legs, let him hobble-jump to his bedroom to change and fall and break his neck.

"I prefer to ensure my subjects are loyal."

"You remove their free will."

He shrugs. "It makes no difference to me."

Keep him talking, Gigi, keep him talking. He's got to possess some sort of conscience. Remember that flash of it you saw earlier? Why else would Brigit have allowed their union?

"Back in Vernal Falls, he was your friend. He helped you fit in at the high school."

He laughs again. I almost throw up in my mouth. Thank the gods my stomach's empty.

"Friend? I don't need friends."

"He trusted you."

He drops to his knees and rests his hands on mine. His gray, lifeless eyes pierce into mine. "You never did. Even when you possessed no memories of your true self, you didn't trust me. Why?"

It was true. I wanted to jump his bones and poke his eyes out.

"Must be your despicable nature."

He leans toward me his lips dangerously close to mine. "You still kissed me. You still wanted me."

"In this reincarnation, I've always indulged in behaviors that aren't good for me. I sank to my lowest when I hooked up with you."

He pushes his lips into mine. I fight to twist away, but it's no use. He's locked on to my lips tighter than plastic wrap and thirty times more suffocating.

Left with one choice, I soften my lips. His tongue slips into my mouth. He shifts to deepen the kiss.

His tongue waggles around, searching for my tongue. Mine plays hide and seek with his, darting in and out. When he shifts all his attention to capturing mine, I chomp down. I wish I had werewolf canines that could really cause some damage. He paws at me to break the hold. I refuse to let go. Rust reaches my taste buds. I almost smile, but then I'd loosen my hold. For now, he's my prisoner, and I'm going to enjoy it.

Finally, he jerks away, holding his mouth. Blood drips from the corners of it.

"Whatsa matter, cat got your tongue?" My blood-stained lips rise into a smile. I relish in my resemblance to the Joker.

His chest heaves in and out. Anger rolls off of him.

Though I know I shouldn't, I can't stop myself. "Did wittle Breas get hurt?"

He flings his blood-covered hand at my face. As it hits my cheek, my head snaps back against the chair. It's the only reason my neck didn't break.

"Ryan," he growls. His tone promises swift and brutal punishment.

Please, I plead silently in the hopes I can break through Ryan's clouded mind.

It's the last thing I remember.

"Gigi," someone whispers. "Gigi, wake up."

I jerk awake. My arms, my legs, my body strain against the chains. My foggy mind begins to remember that I am Breas's prisoner.

"Are you okay?" the familiar voice whispers.

I peer into the blackness and see only the faint hint of golden eyes. "Maddie?"

"Yeah."

"What are you doing here? How did you get in?"

The last time I saw him he was unconscious and tied up outside of Amorin's cottage.

"It appears that my curse allows me to get out of rope— even stuff that burns my hands. And then I followed your scent."

His curse. It bothers me that Maddie doesn't appreciate what he's been blessed with. In the grand scheme of this situation, it really doesn't matter what he thinks of his own abilities, but for me, it does. I didn't appreciate any of my gifts when Gram and Dad first brought them to my attention. If I had, maybe they'd both still be alive.

"You possess a gift. Do not call it a curse."

"Fine, my gift. Can you get out?"

Breas had planned for my vines. That's why Ryan wrapped me with layers of silver chain. But he doesn't know the true strength of my abilities. I'm still learning what I can achieve, and with Gallean's training I have a better handle on mastering it.

I focus on growing vines, but nothing happens. Not even a flicker.

I imagine balls of fire shooting from my palms. Still nothing. Breas warned me that my magic wouldn't work.

I try variations of tricks I learned from Gallean. Nothing works. My head falls back against the chair. My chest heaves against the chains as I try to catch my breath. I'm tapped out.

"The chains are silver. It dampens my magic," I whisper between pants.

"Maybe I can get the key?"

The last thing I want is for Maddie to get caught. He's big. He's powerful. He'd be useful to any side he was on. Breas could compel him into becoming another one of his mindless minions.

"You need to get out of here. Don't worry about me. I'll manage."

"I'll use my curse—er, my gift—to get the key."

He's smart not to mention his abilities aloud. Sometimes it's easy to dismiss Maddie as simple because he doesn't talk much, he isn't obnoxious with an overcompensating fake ego, and he's big and lumbering like Lennie from *Of Mice and Men*, but unlike Steinbeck's stereotype, Maddie goes far beyond expectations.

Not that I want to reside in Breas's prison, but I am curious to find out what he's up to. He's so godsdamn cocky, he'll start blabbering in no time—well, only if his tongue heals.

"Give me a few days, and then, if I don't get out on my own, you can help me."

"I don't know." His eyes shift from side to side. I imagine him wringing his hands together, debating whether to listen to me or to try and free me.

"Go, before you get caught. Search for Alaric."

His eyes still. "He's not here?"

In my gut, I know that Alaric isn't here. The cell doesn't resemble any of my visions, especially since my last one leads me to believe he's in Brigit's shrine along with his father. Besides, I don't feel him anywhere nearby, and though he might now hate me, I love him. I send out my energy just to see if I can taste him, but I'm still empty from my magic chain-wrestling session.

"I don't think Breas has him."

Confusion swirls around Maddie. I can't get a full read on his mind because of the dampened magic, but I sense his emotions.

"But you said . . ."

If he doesn't hurry, he'll wind up getting caught.

"Maddie, go. For Alaric."

His eyes grow into wide orbs. "Someone's coming."

"Go!"

He disappears as footfalls echo down what must be stone stairs. Loud sniffing fills the space.

Oh shit. I forgot about werewolf noses. When Maddie goes invisible, does his scent disappear too?

Ryan flashes a torch in front of my cell. "Who were you talking to?" he snarls, revealing sizable canines. How is he able to partially shift too? Can all werewolves partially shift outside of a full moon, and they just don't realize it?

I swallow in anticipation of the burn that is about to hit

my throat. "Myself. You must remember me talking to myself all the time."

"You're lying."

Never one to miss an opportunity that presents itself, I leap at the chance to keep him talking.

"No, really, I always talk to myself. Who better to have a conversation with?"

He raises his nose into the air and sniffs.

"Do you remember when you first moved to Vernal Falls, and Ms. Lehman sent you to Principal Donahue's office because you asked her a question without raising your hand? And you sat down next to me while I was having a conversation with myself about why Mr. Gagliano kept writing me up for crimes I hadn't yet committed, and you asked me who I was talking to, and I said, 'Myself'?"

He waves the flame around. Thankfully, I don't see Maddie anywhere. He went invisible, but did he heed my advice and sneak upstairs when Ryan got down here, or is he hiding in one of the crevices?

"You remember, don't you? There was that other time that you, me, and Scott picked up Lizzie at the gas station, and I went inside to get her, and while I was walking in, I debated the merits of DC Comics versus Marvel . . ."

His eyes fix on me.

". . . but I was talking to myself, and you snuck up behind me and asked me who I was talking to? And then, Lizzie came up, and you whispered to me, 'Gigi, one day I am going to go out with that girl,' and finally, after almost a year of flirting and dating other people, you did. You remember Lizzie, don't you?"

He blinks.

"Lizzie was my best friend. She was one of the sweetest people in the entire world. There wasn't a mean bone in her body. You two had a lot in common. A lot actually. You're both . . ." I stop myself before mentioning the obvious werewolf thing, "Tauruses so you're stubborn but very kind. You're both . . ."

A blast of light explodes in front of us.

"Silence!" it orders in a disembodied voice neither male nor female.

Ryan's eyes return to black, lifeless orbs. Whatever progress I made with him disappeared with that order, but I made an important discovery. With time I'll be able to switch him back over to my side. I smile to myself. I might be locked in a cell, wrapped in layers of silver chain that quench my magic, but Ryan isn't lost completely.

Neither is Lizzie.

Neither is Alaric.

And who in the gods' name is the owner of that creepy voice?

6

FIVE OF BATONS

Scott had never considered himself a tease, but he supposed that's exactly what he was. If Ryan were still alive and had witnessed what Scott had pulled on Caer last night, he would have punched him in the stomach for being not only cruel but stupid too. Leaving Caer with her eyes closed and her lips anticipating a kiss from him was perhaps one of the lowest things he'd ever done. But then, he wasn't the one who had ripped open a portal and shoved his sister through it. He wasn't the one who had killed a man.

How many men had Caer delivered the death blow to? Why was ending a life easier for her than it was for him? What did that say about him? Or more importantly, what did that say about her?

Sure he had dreamed about her. According to the old myths and legends, she was the Goddess of Dreams. Maybe she had manipulated his. Maybe she wasn't his true love. Maybe the "great" swan relationship was nothing more than a work of fiction written by hopeless romantics, who didn't realize what she really was . . . a murderer.

Since Caer's arrival at the keep, she hadn't been to his room or visited him in his dreams. But then, she had gotten what she wanted—to be trained by Gallean with the singular purpose of destroying Balor. The "dance move" lessons both she and Gigi complained about were over. Now, Scott and Caer spent hours working with knives, swords, hands, and fists. She bested him in many instances, but when he removed his conscience from the training and really concentrated on winning, he bested her—much to Caer's displeasure.

He loved the way her whole body pulsed with power when they were grappling. If he were honest with himself, he had loved the way her lips felt when she'd crushed hers to his even more. And though he tried to talk himself out of the legends that spoke of an Otherworldly relationship, and as much as he tried to dismiss the physical chemistry between them, he knew he'd kiss her again. Her lips demanded his attention.

He paced back and forth in his room. He should probably go out to the courtyard. The room was hardly big enough to contain him, especially at the speed in which he traveled. But leaving his quarters opened up the chance that Caer would show up. He had left her once with closed eyes, tilted chin, and pursed lips. He didn't trust himself to be strong enough to leave her a second time.

He wished he had *The Druid Sisters of Gallicenial* book to distract him. If he could gain insight into Carman's mind, he could find a way to remove her as a threat. While the witch may no longer be in her original physical form (if the wrinkled old lady was actually her first body), it would stand to reason that her actions and motivations would remain the same. She'd continue her vengeful agenda of ridding the world of Brigit. He had to believe that even the darkest, most evil of people had once possessed light. If he could find that light, perhaps he could discover a way to return her to goodness, thereby eliminating her as a threat without any bloodshed.

A novel approach for some. A necessary one for him.

Caer hadn't sleep well. Scott left her longing for him. Again. It wouldn't do to keep thinking about a boy who may or may not be interested in her. He had manipulated her into caring about him—probably to get back at her for the portal incident. She wished he'd put it behind them and focus instead on their training rather than tricking her into wanting to kiss him again.

It had been a mistake to kiss him when she had appeared in Gallean's study. After dreaming about him for so long, she couldn't help herself. She prided herself on self-control, and then she was closing her eyes and puckering up in her bedroom, waiting for Scott to kiss her.

Foolish. Weak. Unattainable.

"Concentrate, Caer," Gallean shouted.

Each day the training had intensified tenfold. Today, Gallean came at them aggressively and without restraint. She tried to parry his assault, but her muscles and her brain were exhausted. Last night, to combat her desire to visit Scott, either in person or through his dreams, she had read *The Druid Sisters of the Gallicenial* and discovered some interesting information about Carman, the witch that Scott seemed to be especially interested in. Carman had betrayed all of humanity when she aligned with Clayone. She threw away her long-term relationship with Ris for the werewolf, or at least for whatever he promised her. The book did not go into details. Carman deserved to die if she wasn't dead already.

"Focus," Gallean growled, swiping at her with bear claws.

Caer leapt away from the extended claws, which narrowly missed her midsection. She'd never seen Gallean partially shift before. Did it mean that he was going to fully shift and she and Scott would be forced to fight the bear, or was it just his way of saying, "Pay attention or I will gut you"? Either way, the claws, along with the rest of the bear, weren't something she wanted to get too close to.

"Pick on someone your own size, hairy," Scott yelled, smacking Gallean's rear end with his sword.

It wasn't like the wizard to leave his backside unattended. Good for Scott to take advantage of the weakness. It was apparently something he excelled at.

Caer ignored the way the area just below her belly button tightened. It would not do for her body to become distracted at the sight of Scott, or any other man for that matter.

She struck at Scott's side, hoping to catch him off guard. He swung his sword down as he twisted away from her. Gallean lunged at Scott's other side. Scott knocked away his attack, constantly shifting his attention between Gallean and Caer, deciding which one posed the most imminent threat. Without any kind of verbal or physical exchange between Gallean and Caer, they both leapt at him at the same time. He'd have to choose one to fight off, thus allowing the other one to attack. Or so Caer assumed.

Scott didn't shift into a bear, a wolf, or any other animal, but he fought them both off as if he had grown a thousand arms. He moved at a speed not of this world. Parrying away their sword thrusts as if they were nothing more than a child's plaything. She had witnessed Scott's speed in the courtyard when he sprinted toward her the day of his arrival, but he hadn't shown any godly powers since then.

But now. Here. He was a god reincarnate.

His speed and battle prowess combined with her skill could bring down Balor's army.

Something bloomed inside Caer.
It wasn't longing for Scott.
It wasn't loneliness or desperation.
It was hope.

What the feck was happening to him? It almost felt like he was losing control of his body, but yet he wasn't. His body had begun to ward off Caer and Gallean's dual attack on its own, but then his mind shifted to command it. He was in complete control of his actions, evolving into something else entirely. He swirled. He slashed. He darted with speed and efficiency, never striking but always at the ready to block off an assault. Gallean and Caer continued to advance, but they no longer proved a threat. In fact, Scott found himself a tad bored and wanted to spice up the situation a bit.

He glanced up at the balcony overlooking the courtyard.
Why not?
He lifted his feet and leapt to the balcony.
Whoa, where the feck did that come from?
He possessed the speed of the Flash, the ability to ward off an attack resemblant of Captain America, and the power to jump like Thor. Adrenaline coursed through his veins. He had become the superhero he'd always longed to be. But instead of being elated, the power surging through his muscles promised to overwhelm him if he lost control.

Gallean and Caer stood with wide open mouths in the courtyard below. Gallean's eyes shone with what Scott suspected was pride. Caer, however, shifted between wonderment and hunger. He didn't know if it was hunger for his new powers, hunger for lunch, or maybe, just maybe, hunger for him. He had left her room last night with her head raised, lips pursed, and chest rising and falling in anticipation of a kiss.

He winked at her, and it was enough to snap her out of her daze. Her long, strong legs took the stairs three at a time. When she reached the landing, she sprinted after him with her sword at the ready. He efficiently evaluated her potential attacks and settled on the most imminent. She feinted to the right, but somehow he sensed that her intention was to attack left and catch him off guard. It wouldn't work. He slipped behind her and wrapped his free arm around her body.

"Gotcha," he whispered.

Catching her had been easier than he expected.

For a second, she leaned into his frame as if she found comfort against him. As much as Scott tried to deny it, he liked having her close to him. He might have wanted to use her for her portal-making ability to get to Gigi, but he did want her all the same. His muscles relaxed as he embraced her. She took advantage of it. She dropped to her knees and spun out of his grasp then leapt back up to a fighting crouch, her eyes now murderous.

It appeared she hadn't forgiven him for last night and planned on punishing him. She'd have to catch him first.

He leapt onto the balcony railing. Her eyes narrowed as she gripped her sword. When her muscles tensed, he ran along the three-inch–wide surface. She chased after him, slashing at his feet with her sword. At each of her attempts, he jumped, and the blade sliced through the empty air as if in slow motion. He skipped along the balcony, enjoying the chase. His balance had always been good, but what he was doing bordered on the extraordinary.

Caer growled in fury. As he rounded the corner, he saw her leap onto the balcony railing behind him. Without even stopping to catch her balance, she sprinted after him, her speed unimpeded by her need to calibrate on the railing. She might as well have been running on flat ground. She was fast —he'd give her that—but he was faster. Her determination at besting him made him realize he'd either have to beat her or have her bow to him. For now, though, he was having far too much fun playing keep-away with her.

He jumped down to the courtyard, softening his knees to land, but he really didn't need to. It seemed his muscles and bones were able to absorb the impact.

Caer screamed in frustration from the balcony.

"Focus, Caer. Remember what you're capable of," Gallean said, his voice reverberating in both their minds and the courtyard.

She froze, staring at Scott, her chest rising and falling as she contemplated Gallean's advice. Suddenly, her eyes shifted as an idea occurred to her, and she smiled.

Scott gaped at her. She was even more breathtaking when she smiled. She didn't do it often, but wow, when she did, she absolutely mesmerized him. He'd been a fecking idiot for leaving her room without stealing one kiss.

In a blink of an eye she was gone. Panic ran through him. Was she in danger? Did she rip her own portal open and leave him?

It wasn't until he heard the scrape of leather boot against stone and felt the jab of her sword against his throat that he realized she had bested him.

"Got you," she whispered, her breath hot on his ear. He leaned into her body, her muscles hard against his back. Electrical currents coursed between them. He had never been so turned on in his entire life.

His nonaggressive, almost surrendering posture seemed to catch her by surprise. Her chest rose and fell with a sharp intake of breath before her teeth ground against each other.

"Concede," she ordered.

But as much as Scott liked having her close, he was still having too much fun.

He whirled away from her and smiled. "You have to catch me first."

7

FIGHT WITH SARCASM

*N*o one came to visit me for what seemed like hours, but it was hard to tell time without a window. Not that I'm complaining. Definitely not complaining. But it's surprising that alpha male Breas didn't return to punish me for biting his tongue. He was probably too busy searching for a witch to cast a magic spell to repair the damage. Too bad I didn't chomp it off. If I had, then unless a witch could cast a growth potion, Breas's tongue's sexual harassment days would be over.

I had spat out the blood that spilled into my mouth after Breas stormed off, but there really was no way to remove it in its entirety, and I had a major case of the heebie-jeebies. I hated having any part of Breas in or near me. If I could cast a spell and remove all remnants of him, I would do it, but alas, the silver extinguished my abilities.

Ryan brought bread and butter for my meal. I refused to eat any of it. My life mantra read like the medieval saying "Cut off my nose to spite my face." Once, when I worried that Alaric and I were a part of an English tragedy, he'd assured me that we were in an Irish story, not an English one. The Irish create their own luck. But sitting in this cell without Alaric, Scott, or anyone I care about feels awfully tragic to me.

I glance at the bread on the plate. Soon the rats would tie on their bibs and sit down for a right jolly picnic in my cell, but I just don't have the stomach to eat anything supplied by Breas. I already feel tainted enough with his blood coursing through my body.

If Scott were here, he'd tell me to eat so I could keep my strength up, but he's off training in the Shadow Realm, most likely pissed off at Caer for opening the portal for me. I do feel bad about that. It wasn't her fault for opening it. She only did what I asked. But Scott will focus his anger about his inability to protect me on Caer. It won't matter that they were paired together in the Otherworld. Scott is stubborn. Not as stubborn as me, of course, but then, not many are.

Without anyone to distract me with either their presence or their mind chatter, I reflect on the vision I had of Brigit's shrine. The place I once thought of as Clayone's tomb. I never considered that just because Clayone couldn't leave his prison, someone else couldn't enter. Would even want to enter. But that appears to be exactly what happened.

The night Alaric disappeared, I assumed Breas took him or somehow cloaked him from my sight. I was blind. I wanted Breas to be the villain. The only villain.

Turns out the world is filled with monsters. And if our world didn't have enough, the Otherworld and the Underworld teemed with them.

But if Breas didn't take Alaric it means that my nightmares, my visions from the Shadow Realm were true, and Lizzie did. She tortured and beat him until he despised hearing my name.

But why would Lizzie align with Clayone? And how did they get to Ireland from Vernal Falls? I know for a fact that

Lizzie didn't have a passport, and even if Clayone had one tucked away in his back pocket, he'd been imprisoned in the church for fifteen years. It would have been way-past expired.

A portal then?

But they'd need a powerful witch, someone like Carman, to allow them passage. And the celestial timing would need to be right—like the night of Samhain. Which I guess is possible . . .

If Clayone could communicate with the outside world while imprisoned in my shrine, it stands to reason that he communicated with people when he was stuck at the church in Vernal Falls. Maybe he wasn't cut off from the rest of the world like Gram, Dad, Clarissa, and the rest of the coven assumed. It's possible Carman and Clayone had communicated with each other all along.

But when he showed up at Brigit's old ruins on Samhain, it didn't seem like he and Carman were on the best of terms. Or perhaps I managed to trick him into believing Carman wasn't telling him her master plan. Could I have compelled him into believing me and distrusting Carman? Was I that powerful? I've seen Scott work miracles with his sweet words. Maybe I possess the ability too.

So, if Carman was helping Clayone, he and Lizzie could have come through the portal together on Samhain. But that still doesn't explain how Breas got to Vernal Falls from the Otherworld or how he returned to Ireland. He didn't take the Gods R Us Express.

When would Carman have had enough power to open a portal from the Otherworld for him? Lughnasadh in August was over. Samhain wasn't until the end of October.

Holy shit.

The fall equinox.

She opened the portal during the fall equinox. Breas

arrived in Vernal Falls in the middle of September. The veil between the worlds would have been close to its thinnest, and if there was a celestial event, it would have been enough power to open it.

But when he arrived on our doorstep, Dad and Gram would have suspected that someone opened the Otherworld door for him. Did they think there was a good witch who opened it? Perhaps Clarissa? She told me that she used a portal to travel to Vernal Falls from Kildare, though it was only open to those from Brigit's bloodline. Maybe they thought she opened one from the Otherworld for him.

That would make sense since they welcomed Breas into our homes without reservation. They even encouraged me to spend time with him. They knew nothing about Breas's relationship with Carman. They didn't know he'd betrayed the Tuatha Dé Danann and had hidden his alliance with the Fomorians as my vision of the day he slaughtered thousands in order to get Brigit to bring her Vessel of Life suggested.

And what about Alaric? I was only aware of Alaric following me in Vernal Falls after Breas had arrived. Based on the way those two acted when they met at the fairy mound in Kildare, they certainly hadn't passed through a portal holding hands either coming or going.

They were both gone by the camping trip though . . .

Something wasn't adding up. There wouldn't have been enough power to open a portal after the fall equinox until the next full moon. There was one at the beginning of October, but that was the night Ryan attacked me, and that was after the camping trip. Breas and Alaric were already gone by then.

I growl in frustration. How did Carman open a portal? I'm still missing something.

Deep breaths, Gigi, deep breaths.

Think.

When Alaric told me about the Sacred Well of Brigit, he'd said that wells and other magical spots used to exist throughout Ireland. Is it possible there's another permanent portal aside from the one for Brigit's heirs? Basically an open door between Vernal Falls and Kildare? That would explain how Clayone had arrived in Vernal Falls when I was a baby.

If this permanent portal does exist, does it allow entrance to other worlds too? And do Clarissa and Granda know about it?

Now back to the Carman-Clayone-possession-of-Lizzie thing. It was Carman who first possessed Lizzie with the eyeball necklace. Carman who led Lizzie to torture Kensey. Carman who pretended to work at the Cathedral's library and befriended me. The witch has been three steps ahead of everyone—gods and supernatural beings alike. During the Super Blue Blood Moon of Samhain, she probably put up a flashing red sign at the permanent portal that said "This Way to the Reincarnated Brigit's Demise."

Carman, that evil witch.

Did she call Alaric back to Ireland because she sensed his growing affection for me? Or because she was worried that if he found out about Clayone, he would no longer be as pliable?

After I took the eyeball necklace from Lizzie, did Carman still have access to her? Was there enough of a connection established that she didn't need a channel to manipulate her? Or was it Clayone who drew her and Ryan to him? It was Ryan's suggestion to go camping, and Breas claimed credit for planting that idea, but Lizzie somehow convinced her parents to allow her to go too, which, looking back, doesn't make sense.

When Clayone bit Lizzie, he took control of her. She was no longer controlled by Carman because Clayone's blood ran through her veins.

Breas somehow managed to compel Ryan even after Clayone bit him, but he's a god so he is powerful enough to spell people, if only for a short time—I learned that lesson the hard way. But Clayone's blood still runs through Ryan's veins.

Blood trumps spells and curses.

What would happen if a werewolf were injected with my blood? Would I be able to return them to human or at least compel them to not want to kill me?

All I need is a needle and syringe.

The only problem is that I'm still locked in a cell and don't have a needle and syringe on my person to test the whole werewolves-who-want-to-kill-me problem.

Without all the mind chatter of others, mine returns to the Breas and Carman situation. Somewhere along the way, they had a falling out. Did it happen back in Vernal Falls? When I slipped into Breas's mind and watched the play-by-play action of the night he almost killed me on the motorcycle, I felt his anger for me after denying him sex. Soon after, his fury exploded when he realized Carman was bewitching Lizzie to keep an eye on him. He almost squeezed the life out of Lizzie. And soon after that, Lizzie tried to exorcise Kensey.

Maybe Carman didn't like Breas trying to usurp her power, and she broke it off with him. That's why he needed a new ally. Someone capable of opening portals. But why Fomorians? Why would he align with monsters for power? Why not call upon his brethren to join his cause?

Then it hits me—because his brethren are Fomorians, the demons who live in the black purgatories of the Otherworld. His allegiance with the Tuatha Dé Danann ended when he betrayed Brigit on the battlefield. The day he slaughtered thousands in hopes that Brigit would bring her Vessel of Life

—which she foolishly did. Which could explain how he intended to bring Fomorians back to this world.

"How does my wife fare?" Breas whispers through the gate, jarring me back to the present.

He just couldn't stay away, could he. He had no issue keeping me locked in the dungeons all by myself with only spelled Ryan as my sole visitor while he recovered from his wounded appendage. Of course, he wasn't aware of my surprise visit from Madigan, who promised to return in two days if he didn't hear from me, but I'm not about to share that juicy information with Breas. For all he knows, I could have swallowed my own tongue and died, and now he dares to call me "wife"? He will bear the brunt of my wrath when I get out of here.

"How's the tongue?"

"Miraculously healed. I assure you Kensey did not find me lacking, but I am not here to gain your affections. I believe that endeavor may be fruitless at the present. In time, however," he says, caressing the lock with his hand and entering the cell, "and with the proper motivation, you'll soon be persuaded that you should align with me, rather than face imminent death." He stops in front of me and puts his hand to the side of his mouth as if to share a secret only with me. "The Witch really doesn't like you."

So a witch then? I can handle a witch.

"Is that supposed to scare me?"

He bends over merely inches from my face. "It should. She's a Fomorian witch."

I flinch from him, but my movements are so restricted by the chains that he could pucker his lips and kiss me. He takes caution though. My attack on his tongue must still loom fresh in his memory.

"If you were to join me, imagine what we could accomplish together," he says in a low, husky, seductive voice. He moves behind me and whispers in my ear. "We could rule the world together. All beings would bend to our will. Serve without question."

"Nobody possesses that power."

"If we reformed our bond, we would dominate all those who tried to rise up against us."

"And why would I want that?"

He whispers in my other ear. "Why wouldn't you?"

"You really don't know me at all."

His fingers trail down my neck over the chains lingering at the base of my throat. "I know you more than you know yourself."

Aware of my vulnerability but unwilling to cow to him, I will not allow him to intimidate me into joining him. "Human beings are precious. They love. They hate. The way they experience emotions should be savored, not destroyed."

His fingers trace my collarbone, a not-so-subtle reminder of his control over my life.

"And what have these precious humans given you other than mockery and scorn?"

An image forms in my mind of elementary school me wearing conservative, boring khaki pants with a plain navy blue collared shirt in an inadequate attempt to blend in with my classmates. My hair's tucked in a low ponytail to try to hide the black hair underneath, but a stubborn patch refuses to remain contained. I watch a cluster of girls, with Kensey leading the pack, pointing at me and whispering, "Skunk Girl." A tear sneaks out. Laughing and pointing ensue.

Another image of me in sixth grade carrying an armload of books and notebooks down the hallway. Someone knocks into me from behind. All my books and notebooks fly across the floor. More laughing. More pointing.

"Cruel. Vicious. Unforgiving. They ought to pay for what they did to you," he hisses.

I shake my head in refusal.

Now, I'm in a frilly pink dress a friend of Gram's picked up at a second-hand shop. The pink flatters my hair and my skin. I actually look pretty. Even the rose corsage on my wrist complements my outfit. Uncle Mark—Dad—bows in front of me and asks me to dance. We swirl around the room, moving in and out of my classmates. A giant smile covers my face. I'm laughing with Dad while other kids whisper and point at me. Kensey stands off to the side of the group with her arms crossed, her dad nowhere to be seen. She glares at her friends—they don't notice her. They were too busy watching me. Admiring me. She follows their gaze and her glare turns glacial when she sees Dad and me. She marches over to the punch bowl, fills a giant cup, and trips into me.

"What offerings do they give you? They only take. They deserve to be punished."

I realize where the memories come from. Sure they're mine, but they're from Kensey. It was Kensey who was cruel and vicious. Kensey who was envious of my relationship with who I thought was my next-door neighbor. Envious of my friendship with Lizzie. With Ryan. With Scott. Our dedication to each other. Our love for one another.

Everyone in my life would die for me. Has died for me.

I may not be able to conduct magic, but I push images into Breas's mind.

Of Lizzie and me playing hopscotch during recess.

Scott and me chasing each other with hoses.

Ryan sitting next to me in Principal Donahue's office and shaking my hand.

Scott and Ryan standing next to me as Kensey mocks me.

Lizzie helping me pick up my scattered notebooks.

Darius dropping me off at home after he found me wandering the flea market by myself.

Gram handing me a mug of tea every morning.

Hugging me when I needed it.

Hugging me when I pretended I didn't.

Dad smiling at elementary school graduation.

Picking me up at school whenever I was sick.

Always being there to help with homework.

Mom sacrificing her life for me.

Gram dying for me.

Dad dying for me.

The sacrifice. The love.

I bombard him with image after image until finally he growls, "Enough!"

"Your efforts are fruitless. I will never turn against my people. There is nothing you can do to persuade me to join your side. To turn against them."

He stomps away from me. "We will see about that," he grounds out as he slams the cell door.

"Nothing will make me change my mind."

He stops and stares at me through the bars, his eyes wild with fury. "You haven't met the Witch."

The awful scrape of nails against stone fills the space between us. Shivers riffle down my spine into my soul.

The Witch is coming.

8

KING OF BATONS

*S*cott had managed to best her in their training session the day before. Even with her going invisible, he somehow sensed her intentions and caught her. It drove her mad.

She watched him move as skillfully and swiftly as Gallean. As if he had spent several lifetimes training rather than just a short time with the wizard. And maybe he had. As a reincarnated god it was possible he had trained as a warrior in the realm from which he came—Earth, as he called it. She felt grossly inept compared to him. She feared that in her early reincarnations she had played the weak female in need of protection.

In response to that thought, her body hummed with strength and power, as if to assure her that was not the case. Her muscles and tendons savored the physical exertion of each training session. Her blood thrummed with adrenaline each time she took a step. She had trained in her past lives. It was as much a part of her as living and breathing. Even as a goddess, she was fierce and intelligent. She felt it in her bones. In her soul.

She watched Scott battle Gallean with his sword with the ruby-encrusted handle. The long silver blade shimmered in the sunlight. It was as much an extension of him as hers was to her. She gripped her own ruby-encrusted handle. Her blade glinted with the morning sun, glowing with the same intensity as Scott's.

How was it that his sword was identical to hers? A mate to her blade. They came from different realms, yet their swords were the same.

Gallean bowed away from Scott's assault. "We shall break our fast before continuing your training."

Scott immediately sheathed his sword. His chest rose and fell with the exertion of his morning exercise. His face shimmered with beads of sweat, and his cheeks glowed pink. His muscles strained beneath his shirt as he hurried to the table. "Good. I'm starving!"

Caer was hungry as well, but much of it had nothing to do with her need for food. She took deep breaths in and out to steady herself. She refused to have something so base as desire dictate her actions. She stood with her sword in her hand as she fought to push away thoughts of Scott, not only of his breathtaking beauty but his magnificent use of the sword as well.

He glanced at her and grinned, his cheeks flushed with exertion. "Are you planning to carve the bread with your sword?"

She blinked and shook her head. As much as she tried to fight her feelings for him, he often left her speechless. Instead of sheathing her sword, however, she rested it on the table to serve as a warning, to herself and to Scott.

Meals tended to be long, quiet affairs with only the sounds of ripping bread and teeth tearing into meat to break the silence. Today, with Scott teasing her, the mood had shifted.

Gallean laid a plate of bread, cheese, and dried meat in the middle of the table. "Scott, it is nice to see that your sense of humor has returned. When your sister was present, your chatter was incessant, but since she's been gone you tend to sit in silence as though your favorite toy was stolen from you."

Scott stiffened as if Gallean had just reminded him that he was supposed to be mad and forlorn. His green eyes flashed at her and a knot hardened in her throat. It was her fault. She was the reason he didn't talk.

"Oh, come now. You can't still hold a grudge against Caer for granting your sister's wish."

Scott's jaw worked as he seemed to consider his next words. Caer felt sick at the prospect of him voicing his anger at her aloud. She barely had control of her emotions now, with his proximity. His words would only confirm what she already knew.

She needed to change the direction of the conversation to avoid his truth.

It had been many years since she'd engaged in topical discussions with guests at a table, but her nursemaid had trained her as a young child in the ways in which to entertain those around her when conversation lacked. She toyed with her sword's handle as she tried to figure out what she would say. She hadn't the faintest clue where to begin.

"Something on your mind, Caer?" Gallean asked.

She studied her sword, careful not to lift her eyes and glance at Scott. "How is it that our swords match? We came from different realms."

Gallean tore off a chunk of bread and slathered it with butter. "When a god reincarnates, his or her symbols of strength manifest in their birth realm."

She thought about that reasoning as she ate some grapes, but that answer did not satisfy her.

"Can they disappear too?"

"No. As long as the lifeblood flows in the owner, the symbolic possession will remain and will always return to the owner."

Scott cleared his throat.

"Yes, Scott?"

"When I was a child, my dad gave me the sword, but it was a small silver dagger. He told me to strap it to my leg whenever I wasn't in school. It didn't change until I fought you—well the bear—in the seomra de rúin."

Gallean laughed before drinking from his goblet.

Scott's forehead furrowed. "What's so funny?"

"You couldn't very well walk around with a giant sword in your world, could you?"

Scott grinned. "I guess not. I would have been expelled from school as a kindergartener."

He spoke about many things Caer didn't understand. It bothered her that there was much she didn't know about Scott and his realm. She tried not to bombard him with too many questions, especially when he spent most of his time ignoring her, but since he was participating in the conversation, she thought she would try one. "What is school?"

Scott's green eyes flashed with amusement. "You don't know what school is?"

He was laughing at her expense, and she didn't appreciate it. "Do not make fun of me."

"No, no, Caer, it just amazes me that in your realm you didn't have school. Gigi would have loved it there. School was her nemesis."

Nemesis she understood. "So school is a monster?"

He bit into a hunk of bread. "To some. To Gigi it was. It's a place kids go to learn."

She eyed her sword. "To learn how to fight? But you said

you would have been expelled from it if you brought your weapon."

"Oh, I would have. And I couldn't have brought the sword as a knife either. School is a place where kids go to learn about science and math, English and social studies."

He continued to speak in words she didn't understand. Did he purposely want to test her patience?

"Explain."

He scratched the scab on his arm from a cut she had given him the other day. At the time she'd felt bad about cutting him when they were merely parrying against each other. Now she was glad she'd done it, especially after their session yesterday and his teasing today.

"To learn how the world works, to learn how to make things, to communicate, to discover answers."

"Like a nursemaid."

He laughed again. "Yes, sort of like a nursemaid, but with desks and chairs, and rules—a lot of rules—along with books and teachers."

"Like Gallean?"

Gallean roared in laughter. "No one is quite like me."

"Agreed," Scott said. "School is a place of education. A place for boys and girls to interact."

She felt a pang of jealously at the thought of Scott interacting with other girls. "Why no weapons?"

"School teaches you how to use your mind so you don't need to use weapons."

"But here you are with your sword, training with Gallean," she said.

He winced, and his eyes turned sad. "Not all enemies can be debated into submission."

"Which brings us to the matching swords," Gallean said, placing his hand on her blade. "May I?"

She nodded.

He lifted the sword and cradled it in both his hands. "These swords were forged by the same swordsmith from the same forge. The blades are made of both silver and iron. The handles include rare stones found only at Lake of the Dragon Mouth, as a tribute to Caer Ibormeith's true home. The swords were given to your godly forms on the day of your union. Caer, yours is named Freagarach, the Answerer. With proper training, it will cut through anything . . . muscle, bone, stone. It is a formidable ally against any enemy."

Caer rolled the sword's name over in her mind, Freagarach—the Answerer. Someday Balor would answer to her. She swallowed as Gallean stroked his palm along Freagarach. She had never let anyone touch it before, let alone hold it entirely and caress it like a lover. Her soul was tethered to that sword, and she wouldn't feel at ease until it was back in her possession.

Gallean, as if sensing her discomfort, nodded as he handed it back to her. Once her hands wrapped around the handle, a thrum ran through it as if coming home. She quickly sheathed it.

"May I?" Gallean asked Scott.

"Of course," Scott said, quickly unsheathing his and handing it over to the wizard. He didn't appear anywhere near as uncomfortable as Caer was when Gallean held hers, but then, Scott always seemed more in control of himself and his emotions.

"Scott, yours is named Moralltach, the Great Fury."

Scott bit into some cheese. "That's what you told me," he said with his mouth full. He swallowed before continuing. "But I thought the blade was only made from silver. It's made of iron too?"

Gallean ran his hand along Moralltach's blade too. Caer watched as an energy shifted between the blade and Gallean's hand, much the same way he had taught them to pull and push energy in their energy dance. It was as if he were examining the sword's entire history rather than simply the elements and artistry of it. She hadn't noticed it when Gallean had held her blade, but then, she was far too preoccupied in her discomfort to observe anything without Freagarach in her possession.

"Indeed. Each metal is capable of killing a variety of creatures, but not all of them. A blade composed of both silver and iron is deadly to every living creature, god or otherwise. The metals tend to be volatile together because of their individual powers. It takes a gifted swordsmith to combine the two. For that reason, there are not many of them in existence, and each one possesses a name to be recognized throughout the ages."

He handed the sword back to Scott. Scott cradled it with new reverence.

"It is a great honor to wield you, Moralltach."

The blade glowed in answer. Caer's eyes widened. She'd never spoken directly to her sword before, though it had been her only companion for many years. Tonight, in the privacy of her room, she'd speak to Freagarach and thank the sword for coming to her.

Gallean sat back in his chair, his arms behind his head. "The swords change to accommodate whatever form you take. So as a human in the Earthly Realm, Scott, your sword becomes a knife, and Caer, as a shapeshifting swan, the sword becomes a necklace."

Scott returned Moralltach to its scabbard. "When I get back to Gigi in Kildare, will it remain a sword, or will it shrink back into a knife? Because a knife isn't going to be much use in a battle with the Fomorians."

"I should clarify. The sword will take the form of whatever shape its owner requires."

Scott dipped his head, awaiting an answer. "So . . ."

"So, if you require a long blade when you return to Gigi, it will remain a sword."

Scott dropped his chin to his chest. "Right."

Sadness filled Caer. Scott was merely biding his time in the Land of Shadows until he could return to Gigi. He'd leave Caer, Gallean, and Balor behind to get back to his sister. A hollowness filled her chest.

Freagarach hummed beside her as if reminding her that she wasn't alone. She patted it before returning to her food. Freagarach would never leave her, and for that she was grateful.

"This afternoon we're going to do something different," Gallean said, rising from the table.

"How do you mean?" Scott asked, sounding unsure about a new approach to their daily schedule.

His unease made her feel better. She wasn't the only one feeling anxious of this new form of training. She hoped Gallean didn't fall back into the energy-pushing routine. That was an absolute waste of time.

Gallean's eyes narrowed at her. He lifted his open palm in the air and blew on it. She shifted out of the way before the energy ball hit her. She remembered all too well the last time Gallean had demonstrated what his energy work could do, and she didn't want to go unconscious in front of Scott. She did not want to appear weak to him, or to the wizard for that matter.

"Do not mock the use of moving energy," Gallean said, "for in many ways Gigi is more powerful than both of your swords combined."

Her gaze shifted over to Scott. He was staring at her. Every time his sister was mentioned, she felt his anger toward her resurface, no matter how light his mood had been.

"This afternoon we need to delve into our minds and outside ourselves to seek answers to Gigi's happenings as well as your own," Gallean said, lifting both of his open palms up and blowing on them.

She winced at the potential onslaught of the energy, but she needn't have worried. The energy lit candles throughout the courtyard.

Gallean knelt down in front of the fire and lit the tip of a sage bundle. As if by magic, the heavy, relaxing scent of burning sage filled the air, instantly loosing her shoulders.

"Now, sit in a comfortable seated position, palms up, and open your throat to the universe."

"Not this again," Scott mumbled.

Gallean ignored the jab. "Breathe in . . . breathe out . . ." he said in a low, hypnotic voice. "Breathe in . . . breathe out . . ."

Caer could not stop thinking about Scott and his proximity to her. She kept switching between wanting to slice his throat with Freagarach and wanting to tug him to her chest and kiss him. Something about his presence awakened a need deep within her that demanded attention. She tried focusing on her breathing. She did not much see the point in turning inward when there was so much happening outward. She shifted in her seat, trying to quiet the building emotion in her, but no matter what position she tried, she could not get her mind off Scott. The incense only heightened the emotion.

She breathed in and out, in and out. Soon the chair and the courtyard disappeared, leaving nothing but cool, damp soil between her toes. She looked around her. The scent of sage hanging in the air suggested she was still at Gallean's keep, but her surroundings hinted she was someplace else. Someplace primordial. An ancient forest. Oak and sweet fern mingled with the sage. She took a step, then another. She kept moving forward and found herself on a path. Desire flooded her veins. She did not question where it came from. She merely acknowledged it and continued forward.

There, in the distance, she saw him. The mighty warrior who had come to claim her as his. She watched him swing his sword and kick at his men enlisted to train with him. She wondered if they came willingly or if they were forced to do so. The blade of his sword did not land on their bodies, even when it would seem it should run them through. His powerful legs and feet knocked them to their knees or on their backs, but still they came at him again and again.

His chest rose and fell with the exertion of the fighting, but he was barely winded even after hours of training. She became so completely enthralled with watching him unabashedly that she wasn't prepared for him to stop training upon seeing her. Their eyes locked, and she could not tear her gaze away.

"My lady," he said, bowing to her.

She pulled her skirts to the side and curtsied.

"What brings you to my training grounds?"

She stepped toward him. His men fell away.

"I came to challenge you."

He threw back his head and laughed. "Challenge me?"

She nodded.

"In your skirts and bare feet?"

"Aye," she said, withdrawing a sword from her back.

He stepped away from her. "I will not fight a woman."

She continued moving toward him. "You will if you want to win my hand."

He swallowed, clearly unnerved. Good, she would use it to her advantage.

She lifted her sword above her head and charged at the warrior. His green eyes widened. He lifted his sword, not to combat her but to ward her off. She came at him again and again. Still he refused to retaliate.

"Fight me," she growled.

"I will not attack you."

"I do not want you to attack me. You must prove to me you are my equal in every way before I will consider your hand."

He glanced at his men. They eyed him warily.

"Fight me, or you are a coward!" she shouted, jabbing his waist with her sword to prove she would wound him if he refused.

He finally took a combative swing. She knocked it away as if it were nothing more than a moth in daylight. He came at her again and again. She parried his onslaught. Her heart pounded in her chest. She had never felt so alive.

His eyes glowed with excitement as his swings increased in strength.

She did not find him lacking. For that reason, hope bloomed within her. Perhaps he was the mate foretold to her. Her equal in every way but one.

She fought off his advance. Somewhere in their dance he had shifted to the aggressor. She stumbled on the folds of her dress but righted herself quickly.

"I told you those skirts would be the death of you."

"Fear not, for I wore them merely to distract you." With one swift motion she untied the skirts and fanned them out in front of the warrior, obscuring his view.

His sword tore them away. "I never thought it would be so easy to disrobe you."

"Do not flatter yourself with ego, for it is I who is in charge of this battle."

"I didn't think we were fighting. I thought this was a dance." He feinted to the left. She anticipated it and leapt to meet him, but it was the movement he intended. He wrapped his arm around her body and pinned her to him.

"Do you yield?"

"Never," she grunted, ducking out of his hold, but the warrior was faster. This time she found his sword point sticking in her neck.

"Do you yield?"

She considered her options. Somehow it was she that had become distracted and given away her upper hand.

"Yes," she said reluctantly.

"Good," he said, pulling her toward him.

Her chest rose and fell. The warrior had proven himself worthy of her affections, but she refused to yield entirely. She wrapped her hands around him, pinning his arms to his sides as she met his lips with her own. His hands soon found her waist. They pressed against each other.

A dull ache blossomed within her. She needed the warrior to quell it.

"Is this real?" she whispered.

"I certainly hope so," he replied.

"Caer," a voice tickled in her ear. "Caer, wake up."

9

SCARY-ASS WITCH

a hard cold pushes out any warmth left in my veins. All the remaining goodness in my soul has been ripped away, replaced by an absolute certainty that death is coming. Mine. Scott's. Everyone's.

I'm scared. There, I admit it. I'm scared shitless.

As if a phantom, the Witch lingers in the shadows, tormenting me by the mere thought of her appearance. When I'm certain I will crumble from fear, she steps out from the shadows, and my world turns on its head.

"Kensey?"

A leer emerges from my nemesis's face. A leer more evil, more terrifying than any Kensey has ever given me.

"I don't understand."

She scrapes her long nails up and down the iron bars of the cell. Cold dread circles and whirls around her. I always thought Kensey was the devil incarnate, but this witch, this Fomorian being, is more horrifying than my worst nightmares (and my nightmares would scare the hair gel out of an Elvis impersonator). Even Carman, a Maleficium sorceress, didn't scare me. But this . . . this being in the form of my sworn enemy causes me to question every single one of my life choices.

Her hair's wild. Not brushed. Not combed. Not washed. Yet no bird would make a nest in it. No bird could get close enough to build one. The toxic air swelling around her would mean instant death for any living being. Wind would fear to whip through her tresses for chance it would be slashed by the jagged razor points.

And her eyes. Her soulless, lifeless eyes. Dead snake eyes.

If Kensey knew what this Fomorian witch had done to her appearance, she'd make a deal with Derg himself to combat her.

"What have we here?" Fomorian Witch Kensey hisses.

I wait for the forked tongue to dart out and in, but I can't let this . . . this thing know I fear it. She eats fear.

"Who are you?"

"You know who I am."

I will not give her what she wants. I will not feed her hunger.

"I assure you, I don't."

"We once fought together."

I try to remain expressionless, but my wide eyes must give me away. She doubles over, cackling at what must be a joke, though I find nothing funny about it (and I pride myself on my colorful personality).

Control, Gigi. Control.

"We did?"

"Well, we fought against each other."

"Who won?"

Her eyes narrow into slits. "We never finished."

My stomach roils at the implications of her answer, but I must be brave. I must appear confident.

"Pity."

"Your union to Breas ended the war." The bitterness in her answer ices the air in the cell.

"Sorry about that."

"Soon we will resume where we left off."

I indicate the layers of silver chains around my arms and legs. "It appears I'm indisposed."

She reaches her hand into the cell. She's at least ten feet away from me but her arm stretches across the empty space between us. I pull my head back. I want to close my eyes to shut out the entire situation, but it's like a gruesome scene in a horror movie—you don't want to look but you have to. Sharp fingernails drag across my face. Blood pools at the gashes before overflowing and seeping down my cheek. Soon it trails to my neck, sizzling as it hits the chain, whether from the contamination of the Witch's nails or because of my own blood, I don't know.

The chains begin to warm as the blood hits them, growing more and more uncomfortable around my neck. Without the ability to lift them off my skin, I start to panic.

"What did you do to me?"

"Chains, even those made of silver, wouldn't stop a truly magical being," she hisses. "This form is weak. There will be no challenge when we fight, but a win is a win."

Of that, I have little doubt, but when would such a war be waged? Does she plan to battle me while I'm chained in the cell, already rendered defenseless by the magic-dampening silver?

The chains grow hotter, searing my neck.

"Stop, please stop," I beg, unable to raise my voice for fear that the hot chains will further damage my vocal cords.

She throws back her head and cackles in answer.

The pain becomes unbearable. "Please," I moan. Tears stream down my cheeks, mingling with the tainted blood. But the burning sensation fades as the tears reach my neck. I almost cry out in relief, but I don't want the Witch to know her torture has ended. "Please," I whisper faintly.

"Enjoy," she says as she climbs the stairs. Her laughter echoes down to me long after her departure, until it finally fades. A heavy, uncomfortable silence remains.

The burning lessens as more tears mingle with the blood. On the night of Samhain, after I returned to the tower to free my dad and was imprisoned with him instead, he and I almost paid the ultimate price for my inability to listen to his request for me to stay away. Those tears I shed grew powerful vines. Vines capable of strangling the guard. Vines capable of pulling apart thick rope. Those powerful vines were the reason why Breas used layers of silver chain link this time, but the Fomorian witch said that truly magical beings would not be inhibited by the silver.

In the tower, I had Dad to save. He was my inspiration, my desperation to free myself and him. Now it's just me. A being who wants to live above all else but doesn't know if she can continue to do so with all her family gone, with Alaric aligned with Clayone, with Lizzie and Ryan against her.

I tug and pull on the layers of chains. Tears continue to mingle with the blood. Soon the chains no longer burn. In fact they feel almost pliable. My arms and legs can move. Not a lot, mind you, but more than they could before. There's only the chain at my neck that still binds me without forgiveness. I swallow, preparing myself for the inevitable pain before extending my neck forward. The links bite into my skin, but I keep pushing forward. I can feel my throat constricting with the effort, but I don't need to breathe. Not right now. Right now I need to free myself. When I'm free I can breathe all I want. I push and push against the tight chains. Not swallowing. Not breathing. Just pushing. Just pulling.

The chains stretch into thin strands of liquid metal until

I'm almost standing. Just as I'm ready to free myself from these binds, I hear it.

A whimper.

A sigh.

Lizzie.

I collapse back against the chair, panting with the effort. My breath takes too long to regain itself. Too long until I can take a normal breath, a quiet breath, a breath that will allow me to hear who might be in the cell next to mine.

Another quiet whimper.

Another audible sigh.

"Lizzie?" I whisper into the darkness.

A sharp intake of breath.

"Lizzie, is that you?"

No answer. But in the silence, I recognize the truth. My best friend is locked in the next cell.

I close my eyes and focus all my energy on reading a mind I know better than my own, or at least thought I did. Back in Vernal Falls, Ryan and Scott had revealed another side to my Lizzie that I never knew existed. A side fiercely protective of her best friend.

There's also that other side. The one from my visions that tortured Alaric every time he called out my name. The one possessed by Carman. The one obsessed with a spell book. The one working for Clayone.

But if she's working for Clayone, why is she here?

I close my eyes and focus on her mind. Poison courses through it. Carman. Clayone. Breas. Too many villainous beings have corrupted her mind. Lizzie, my Lizzie, is lost somewhere inside their insidious web. I take a deep breath to steady myself, to build my strength and concentrate on purging her mind of the containments. The hate bestowed upon her from the three evils forms a thick, impenetrable layer. The unifying source, the common thread of all the sources, is hate for me. Both human girl and goddess.

I poke at it, try to manipulate it, but it is unyielding. The effort leaves me gasping for breath. I refuse to give up. I won't. There must be some way to cleanse her of this bottomless chasm of loathing.

Again and again I work to eradicate the evil to no avail. Panting with the effort, I throw everything I have at it, but nothing seems to weaken the surface.

It is too much for you, Gigi. You must gather your energy. Do not weaken yourself, for you may not be able to regain your strength.

I ignore Brigit's warnings. It's Lizzie we're talking about. Poor sweet Lizzie. And I will deplete myself to my very last breath to save her.

I concentrate all my focus, all my energy on her mind. Finally, I'm able to enter. I probe it, searching for any positive images of me, but I only find me doing bad things. Me corrupting her by having her skip school. Me stealing some gum at the gas station and shoving it in her pocket. Me talking her into sneaking out of her house and driving her parents' car to Pittsburgh when we were fifteen. Every terrible thing I've ever done to her attacks me, bombarding me with memory after memory.

The visions grow fuzzy around the edges. I fight to remain awake. The chains are suffocating me. I can't breathe. I can't . . .

Standing at the edge of the meadow, I savor the sunshine warming my face. Foxglove, bee balm, and rudbeckia bend toward the light. My fingers brush along the tips of them. Energy flows in me and to me. There, on the far side of the pond closest to the church, nearest to Clayone, stands Lizzie. *The sun doesn't reach that side of the meadow. It's steeped in darkness. I reach out my palm and extend a ball of light out. Just as it reaches Lizzie, it bounces back to me.*

The pond stretches the expanse between us. Though no wind blows, the water swells and roils as if a great storm wages within it. The only way to reach Lizzie is to cross the water. This I know.

I dip a toe in. As the tip penetrates the surface, my skin sizzles from the poison water. There must be some way to cross the pond. There must be some way to bridge the gap between us.

On a small island halfway from either side sits a carved mahogany box. Inside lies the answer to getting Lizzie back. To regaining her trust. I call forth to the box and try to bring it to me to no avail. A sense of urgency prickles the back of my neck. Danger is coming. If I remain here much longer, I will be lost, but I will not leave Lizzie. I will not forsake her.

Desperate, I search the shoreline for a boat or log to use. The only way for me to save Lizzie is to reach the box.

The darkness surrounding her begins to creep across the pond. The evil cannot take her.

"My light, my love, my life," my mother whispered to me before she lifted her hands up and walked across the water.

I lift my hands and step onto the water. Lizzie's eyes widen as I take another step and another.

She screams, "Noooooo!" over and over. Worse than a banshee. Worse than anything ever uttered by any living being.

So loud. So awful. It could wake the dead.

It awakens me.

My eyes spring open as I gasp for breath. The chains no longer bite into my neck and chest. I can draw in a long, full breath. I can't gulp in enough of the sour dungeon air to fill my lungs. When I've finally gotten my fill, I fall back against the chair.

Never have I come against anything so bitter. So unyielding.

"Lizzie," I whisper, trying once more.

When there's no response, I listen for her breath. The long, slow inhale and exhale of sleep fills me with hope. I reach out to her mind. I can't fully penetrate it yet, but there's a definite softening. Ryan rises to the surface of her mind—that's how Breas caught her. He wanted to use her to get to me.

I am the reason.

It's always been me.

All those years ago when I so desperately needed a friend, Lizzie came to me. I cherished her as a gift. Tried to protect her. To keep her safe. But all Lizzie's memories tell a much different story.

I did this to her.

I caused her death.

I caused her rise.

I would have been nothing without her, but without me she would have been free from the evil poisoning her.

I killed Lizzie.

I killed them all.

I am not worthy of their sacrifice.

Gigi, you are worth it, my mother whispers in my ear.

Gigi, you are worth it, Gram whispers in my other one.

Gigi, you are worth it, Brigit whispers with absolute certainty.

The babe. The maiden. The crone. The circle of life.

No beginning. No end.

Always existing. Always continuing.

From the end, comes the beginning.

My fingers in the earth. My toes in the dirt.

Vines wrapping around me. Embracing me.

Gram and Mom watching with wonder.

The sun warming my face.

The sky, a brilliant blue, without hint of storm.

Tiny shoots sprout deep beneath the earth, growing with speed and strength. Breaking through bricks and stone in search of their goddess. Winding in and around the chains. Slipping through the links. Forming a protective layer between the chains and their goddess. Expanding upward and outward until the chains disappear into nothing.

I step through the wall separating us as if the stones and mortar are nothing more than air. I take hold of her hands. If she should awaken, it is too late for her to resist.

She falls. I fall.

Memories of the night of the campfire come flooding back to me. The laughter. The stories. Our introduction to Clayone and werewolves, along with the discovery that witches, werewolves, and magic are real. Lizzie walking hand in hand with Ryan. An aura generates from them. I dwell on the image. Warmth permeates off of Ryan, but even free from the eyeball necklace, the spell book, and Carman's possession, darkness drifts off of Lizzie.

I focus in on the memory to see what was hidden from me before. And there it is in the briefest of instants. Her eyes flash gold and red. Lupine eyes, but not the pure gold ones of Alaric. Hers demonstrate the mingling of good and evil. My worst fear has come true. My best friend, at least the Lizzie I thought was my best friend, is dead all over again.

The scene of the four of us wandering into the church unfolds before me. I hover above, watching it as an observer. Lizzie whispers in Ryan's ear. His green irises disappear, replaced by black. He reaches up for the crumbling ceiling and pulls it down. They laugh as Scott and I scream before we realize what happened. After brushing the debris off, I haul off and punch Ryan in the gut. He doubles over, gasping for breath. A pang of guilt for hurting him washes over me, but it's soon replaced with surprise as Lizzie's eyes flash red. How had I missed that? Who was Lizzie really?

Lizzie's hand hovers over the symbols on the walls as she wanders down the hallway. Almost touching, but not quite. Someone, Ryan maybe, says, "I betcha devil worshippers came up here." But the symbols aren't from any type of dark magic. They're ancient runes to ward off evil spirits. I recognize them now, though at the time I was too caught up in the moment to realize their origins. Lizzie's fingers begin to trace a rune. She jerks away from it, wincing, just as Scott and I slip past her and wander into the main cathedral room with its high ceiling and painted floor.

Lizzie's eyes flash red again as she takes in the room. Ryan remains by her side, his eyes returning to black orbs.

I watch myself twirl three times in one direction as I call out, "Do you know what this is?"

My stomach roils, and I swallow the vomit filling my mouth as I watch myself switch direction. All our lives would be irrevocably changed in the next turn. I glance over to see Lizzie and Ryan tucked safely behind Scott as he warns me we should get out. As I round my third circle, Lizzie grabs Ryan's hand, and they leap into the center of the room as the floor explodes.

She jumped on purpose.

You fall. I fall.

Gasping, I pull out of the memory and return back to Lizzie's cell. I had put all the blame for that night's events on myself. I believed with all my heart and soul that I killed Lizzie. That I killed my best friend.

But I didn't kill her . . .

"You saved me," she whispers to me from her curled-up position on the floor, her eyes flashing red.

"What are you?"

"I am a servant of the darkness."

"You are not a servant of the darkness. You're Lizzie. My Lizzie."

"The darkness created Clayone."

"No, Derg did."

"My parents worshipped the darkness."

Somewhere along the way she slipped into a zombie-like trance. My magic isn't able to repel it, but maybe my words can.

"Your parents were Jehovah's Witnesses."

"My parents worshipped the ancient ways, Druidry and witchcraft with your gram's coven."

I had read in Dad's journal that Lizzie's parents were friends with my mom. If they were friends with her, they were probably also friends with . . . no, it can't be.

In a lame attempt to rewrite the story, I say, "Your parents left the coven because they were worried that my power would hurt you."

She throws back her head and cackles just like the Fomorian witch. Just like Breas. What's with the evil laughter, anyway? Is it a prerequisite for admission to the diabolical planning club?

"Your parents were friends with Calliope, weren't they."

She grins widely at me.

Carman trained them. I'm sure of it. That's how she so easily possessed Lizzie, even without the eyeball necklace. That's why Lizzie became obsessed with the spell book. It was Carman who introduced her parents to Maleficium. But something still doesn't fit.

"What about Clayone? How does he play into all this?"

"I am marked as his," she says.

That's not creepy or anything.

"What the fuck does that mean? Are you his concubine? His lover? His . . ."

Oh my gods.

It's now Lizzie squeezing my hands. "Say it, oh wise goddess. Say who I am."

It hurts to look at her, but it hurts to say the truth even more. "You're his daughter."

A twisted grin appears on her face.

"You knew all along, didn't you."

She winks.

After my come-to-Goddess-Brigit moment in my cell, I'm too pumped with adrenaline and purpose to let Lizzie or anyone else win. Besides, she's really starting to piss me off with that maniacal glint in her eyes and her depraved smile.

"Our friendship was not a lie. It was real."

Her eyes flash red. "Your entire life was based on lies. Why should our friendship be any different?"

Her words kick me in the stomach. I double over, unable to breathe. "What about Ryan? Did you care about him at all?" I whisper with halted breath.

Her eyes shift from red to gold at the mention of Ryan.

Realization dawns on me. "That's how you got caught, isn't it."

She closes her eyes, and the cell falls back into blackness. The only noise is her bated breath.

I kneel down with her hands still in mine, willing her to look at me. I can reach Lizzie, my Lizzie, if she'd just look at me. A boot scrapes against stone. My ears tingle at the sound. I concentrate on forming an image in my mind. The Witch, Breas, or Ryan? One wants to kill me, one wants to possess me, and one was one of my best friends. The unknown visitor snarls.

Lizzie grips my hands, pulsing with excitement.

Ryan then.

Fists bang against the cell. "Goddess, where are you?" he growls into the neighboring cell.

When I don't answer, he unlocks the door and stalks in. I loathe to leave Lizzie, but if Ryan discovers I'm missing, all will be lost.

"Ryan, I'm here," I whisper, careful not to raise my voice and alert Breas or the Witch.

He sucks in his breath, slamming the cell door behind him. He sniffs as he approaches Lizzie's cell. I can just make out the shadow of his form in the darkness.

Lizzie's hold tightens. She still cares. At least for Ryan, anyway.

"What are you doing here?" his voice rumbles through the bars.

I pull Lizzie up as I stand.

"Ryan, did you know Lizzie was in here?"

He falters backward. His sharp intake of breath suggests he didn't.

"Didn't you smell her?"

He inhales deeply. "I thought I smelled her, but she was dead . . ." his now-gold eyes flash over to me, "and you killed her."

My goddess compelling didn't work with Lizzie, but maybe it could work for Ryan. "I didn't. She's here now. I can take both of you with me."

His fingers curl around the bars. "You speak treason."

In a calculated move, I release my grip on Lizzie and grab Ryan's arm through the bars.

He snarls, "Release me, Goddess, or I will alert my master."

"He is not your master," I hiss and thrust my face between the bars so I'm inches from him. The movement is so fast, so unexpected, he doesn't move. "No one is your master."

"No one is my master . . ." he says.

"No one is your master, and you will open the cell."

He slips one hand into his pocket and withdraws the key. "No one is my master, and I will open the cell."

As his key clicks into the lock, snake-like smoke circles around us and slams us together into the bars of the cell.

"You will not escape," the smoke snarls in the Witch's voice.

Lizzie gasps as we're pressed harder into the bars, unable to move. Ryan is pinned against them on the other side.

Breas laughs from the top of the stairs. "Your magic will not work here, Goddess."

His cocky attitude unfurls my anger. Power surges through my limbs. "You don't know what I am capable of," I roar, thrusting myself away from the bars but still retaining my grasp on Ryan and Lizzie. I envision the crescent moon garden I created at Granda's, the restorative quality of the herbs I planted there along with the protective enchantments I remembered from *Briguathe Grimoire*. "And you best remember that."

The three of us fall through the portal together.

You fall. I fall.

THE MOON

*C*aer sat at the windowsill. Again Scott had witnessed her weakness, this time during their meditation when she fell into a dreamlike trance starring him as Oegden. She despised appearing weak in front of anyone, let alone the man she was allegedly joined with in the Otherworld. The whole union thing confused her, though she figured that would explain her body's unfamiliar responses whenever he stood near her. It certainly had nothing to do with his beauty or his fighting skills or the timbre in his voice that tickled her in unaccustomed places.

For the most part, he ignored her, refusing to demonstrate any warmth for her except for his playful interactions over the past two days, but she was not a fool. She did not believe he was softening to her. In fact, if she was honest with herself, she thought that he might be manipulating her. He had made his desire to get back to Gigi well known, and Caer possessed the means to get him there with her portal creation. It didn't matter if they were paired together in the Otherworld. The legends, the myths could be wrong. Besides, they were written by the winning side.

There was little mention of Caer Ibormeith, Goddess of Dreams, Sleep, and Prophecy anyway. What did dreams and prophecy mean in a world at constant war? Nothing. Absolutely nothing.

It was no wonder Scott didn't harbor true feelings for her. She was a plague. A short footnote in the history books.

Tears wet her cheeks as she stared out into the black night. She had been wrong to come here. Wrong to reveal herself to Scott and Gigi. Wrong to rip open the portal for Gigi. She had been wrong about so many things. She'd spent almost a lifetime isolated from any human interaction.

During her solitude she had never acted impulsively. She planned and she plotted—which was the reason she had returned to Gallean's keep after he expelled her. She needed help to fight Balor and figured Scott would be as strong an ally as any. And she was correct in her assumption. Over and over again he had proven himself useful in battle. His speed. His skill with a blade. His determination. He would be invaluable in a fight. She planned to use him for her own purposes. In truth, she was as wretched as he was. Two selfish beings could never align out of such a weakness as love.

She closed her eyes. Tiredness pulled at her muscles. Since returning to Gallean's keep, she felt chained. She hadn't been rooted to a place since she was a faerie princess, and that life was forsaken so long ago she barely remembered it.

Her arms twitched for flight. Her heart ached for freedom. She climbed onto the windowsill and glanced back at the room. The soft feather bed she'd grown accustomed to, and the piles of books and objects strewn across every flat surface had provided her with the means to pass the time, but still she missed the wind under her wings. If she could fly next to the moon once more . . .

Her training had neared its completion. There wasn't

much more the wizard could teach her. Besides, Scott was a constant distraction. He might be a worthy warrior, but in a fight for her life, she couldn't lose focus. It was time for her to soar.

The skies called to her, their beckoning irresistible. She stepped out of the window and took flight.

Guilt ate at Scott. The yearning in Caer's eyes filled him with longing. It was wrong to use her for the sole purpose of getting back to Gigi. What would his dad say? Or Gram for that matter? He was wrong to use his true love, his soul mate, to get back to his sister. It was equivalent to his mom's action when she had told Clayone Gigi's whereabouts—sacrificing one for another. As much as he'd like to forgive his mother, the very fact that she had betrayed her family in order to protect him proved little consolation. Was he his father's son or his mother's?

Gigi had a mind of her own. Though she'd never admit it, she always got what she wanted (once she figured out what she wanted).

The woven rug in his room couldn't keep up with his godly pacing. A normal human wouldn't wear a hole through the wool within only a few hours, but a god, even a reincarnated one, could.

He was sure that Gallean knew what he was planning. He'd seen it during their meditation this afternoon. Scott had injected himself into Caer's mind. In her godly form she may be the Goddess of Dreams and Prophecy, but in her reincarnated human one at least, her dreams could be manipulated. The wizard had said nothing, but the very fact that he saw Scott's scheme was cause enough for even more guilt.

As his stomach churned with enough acid to take down a pack of hellhounds, he left his room to confess his intentions to Caer and ask for her forgiveness. If there was going to be any future for them in this world or the Otherworld, the truth about his ulterior motives must be confessed to her.

He knocked at her door before he even had time to think about what he would say to her or to second-guess himself. He waited for her welcome but when none came, he stood outside her room, unsure how to proceed. If it were Gigi in there, he'd burst in after a brief knock, but with Caer, there were too many walls built around him to enter without an invite. After a deep breath, he knocked again.

Still no answer.

He lifted the door latch and announced his arrival—only there was no one there to hear it.

"Caer," he called out, searching the room for her. "Caer?" He looked under the bed and behind the tapestries, unwilling to acknowledge the open window. But when a soft breeze caressed his cheek, he had to admit the truth.

She was gone.

Scott climbed onto the windowsill and stared out at the night sky. He was a fool. An absolute fool.

Gigi would call him an idiot, or more likely, a fecking idiot.

Ryan would shake his head and tell him that he had blown his chance. Then, with a wink, he'd say, "There are other fish in the sea. In fact, there are many, many seas, all loaded with fish."

But the one Scott wanted, the one he needed, was a swan in the sky. He imagined what it would be like to soar through the air with the wind beneath his wings. A keen yearning for Caer consumed him as he stared out into the darkness. A fat tear slid down his cheek. He reached up to brush it away, but instead of a hand, a wing swiped across his skin. He blinked to double-check what he was seeing. Feathers poked through his pores. His face pinched and tightened.

He gasped, but no human voice came out. It was replaced instead by a squawk. He twisted his head from side to side, no longer able to see directly in front of him. What was happening to him? Did Gallean slip something into his tea?

Terror struck through him. In this form he was weak, unable to protect Gigi or Caer, unable to protect anyone.

In this form you are powerful.

The wind called to him, and he answered.

He stepped into the night. He'd find Caer. He'd find her and bring her back, and if he couldn't convince her to return, he'd remain with her.

A sudden gust caught his wings and shot him into the night sky. His transition was complete. He soared through the air. Freedom pulsed through his veins. Never in his life had such a rush of adrenaline raced through him. He felt so, so alive.

Scott swept down into the lands outside Gallean's keep—the very ones Gigi and he had walked across when they arrived in the Shadow Realm. The very ones Caer had strode across to watch them train. Caer wore her loneliness like a curse. It was a blessing. A gift.

An updraft lifted him away from the ground and toward the heavens. There, in the distance, he saw her. He had never seen her in her swan form, but he knew her spirit. He knew her, and he was an idiot—a fecking gobshite—to ignore his feelings for his soul mate.

She heard the rush of flapping wings. She didn't think her flock could find her in the Shadow Realm, but perhaps her flight had signaled her swan form and they could pass

93

through different realms to receive her. She slowed to allow them to catch up and glanced back. A single swan approached her. She instantly recognized Scott.

What was he doing here, and how had he turned into a swan? If he tried to stop her, she'd fight him in the air. She didn't have much experience with flying, but she had more than he did. She planned her assault as he approached. He slowed his wings to match hers. She glanced back at him and he winked before stretching his neck and flying above her. But instead of attacking, he glided through the air in a circle before joining back up with her. He nodded his beak, encouraging her to try. Instead she dipped her beak and plunged into a steep dive, only pulling up just before hitting the ground. Exhilarated, she met back up with him. They circled and plunged side by side in perfect synchronicity with each other. Together they crested the boundary of Gallean's place and continued over the long valley in the direction of the village. Never had she felt so alive. A song sprang in her throat. Scott also opened his beak to sing, but before a note could be sung, the beating of large wings filled the air above them. Before either of them could react, a giant bird gathered them beneath its wings and pushed them toward the earth. It pulled up just in time for them to land.

In front of Caer and Scott stood the largest eagle she'd ever seen with striking amber eyes. Why were they familiar to her? And more importantly, why had it tried to kill them?

Caer shifted quickly back to her human form, her sword held at the ready. Scott mirrored her actions, he, too, bearing his sword. The eagle blinked at the swords, unimpressed with their sharpness, unfamiliar with their names or their legacies. Perhaps if it felt the blade as she tore off a wing?

It will do no good.

"Gallean?"

The eagle shifted back into the wizard.

"What are you doing here?" she asked.

"I can ask you the same."

"You can shift into an eagle too?" Scott asked in wonder.

"I can take whatever form I desire. The bear strikes fear with invaders to my keep. The eagle overpowers little birds that sneak away from their nest."

Caer lifted her chin. "A swan is not little, nor did I sneak away from your keep. I left on my own free will."

Scott stepped toward her. "Why did you leave?"

Her eyes watered as she stared at him. She would not admit her shortcomings to anyone.

"I did not grant you leave," Gallean said.

She cleared her throat as she puffed out her chest with her sword at the ready. "I was unaware I had to ask permission for such matters."

Before an answer could come, the very ground they stood on shook.

"Earthquake!" Scott said.

"No," Gallean said as he rushed toward the outskirts of the village, his cloak billowing in the wind, "Balor's army is attacking the enchantments of my boundary shield."

"To your keep?" Scott asked, his eyes locking on Caer's, wild with worry.

"No," Gallean shouted, his battle fury spilling over as he ran. "To the entire island. You two must leave. Your time here is over."

Caer chased after him with Scott in close pursuit. "We will not abandon you or the island. We will fight."

"It is not time," Gallean roared. Soon he'd be unrecognizable if the bear took hold.

"It is time when I say it is time," Caer growled as she and Scott ran alongside the wizard.

"Besides," Scott said, somehow sounding relaxed in this

time of stress, "you have no army to support you. You need us."

Gallean cracked his neck, fighting to keep the bear under control. "I can keep them busy long enough for you to get away."

Caer slipped her sword back into its sheath. She could move faster if she wasn't holding it. "I will not run from battle. I do not shrink from war. Fear will not swallow me."

A blast split the very earth between their feet. Scott and Caer leapt over the opening, knocking into each other.

Scott reached for her. "Maybe Gallean is right. Maybe we should leave."

She veered away to avoid his touch. She would not be distracted. "Gallean needs us."

As if to prove her point, dozens of men, women, and children ran screaming from their huts, filling the already chaotic streets.

"I will persuade the villagers to join our cause," she shouted. "Their lives are in danger too. They are my people."

Gallean swiped his claw at her. "You're people? They are no warriors. They are people without homes. Runaways, orphans, thieves . . . they live in the in-between."

Caer's muscles tensed as she swerved away. "Is that not what I am? Did I not live alone for years without even a wizard as company? I watched these village children grow. I raided their homes at night for bread and cheese. Their presence soothed me. Even when I was invisible amongst them, I felt a part of them."

Scott tried to reach for her again, but she would not be deterred.

"Caer, this is madness. You are a powerful woman. I am a powerful man. But even with the villagers, we are no match for Balor's army."

Power swelled within her. "I am Caer Ibormeith. I am the

Goddess of Dreams and Prophecy. That's why these people came to the Shadow Realm—to live a dream, even if it was not their best one—and I will unite them."

She broke away from Scott and Gallean and strode into town. She gathered her courage as she walked. She remembered the way her father spoke to his people—rallied them, encouraged them, stood by them. She would do the same.

"People of the Shadow Realm, I have come to unite you against a common enemy."

The barmaid from The Howling Wolf tavern called out, "I remember you. Keegan left with you and was found dead moments later."

Caer flustered at the reminder. At the time, her need for Scott had superseded her common sense, and she had sought satisfaction from a stranger as a substitute. The man had groped her and tried to take her after she'd changed her mind and told him no.

She could lie and pretend it didn't happen, but that was the coward's way and she was no coward. Gallean had told her that.

"I killed him."

Scott's forehead bunched as he glanced at her. Good. He should fear her as well. She was a mighty warrior.

The barmaid spat on the ground. "The bastard deserved it. With his pretty face, he thought he could treat women like garbage, like they were his property."

Other women stepped forward and clapped. "Aye," they agreed.

Caer seized the opportunity. "Balor's army is coming."

The barmaid brandished two knives from behind her back. "I have not heard that name for many years. How is it that he can enter the Shadow Realm? I thought we were safe here."

Caer recognized the longing for safety in the barmaid's voice. She had cried it herself many nights for many years.

"There is a sickness upon the boundary. Balor wants me."

"I say we give her to him and be done with it," a short man cried. He had been Keegan's companion. The coward.

Scott stepped in front of Caer. "Try it and I will strike you down."

The barmaid along with three other women shoved Keegan's friend into a pile of compost meant for the pigs. "You belong with the swine, you milksop."

"I say we help!" one of the women yelled.

The ground shook again.

"Of course we will."

"My energy stores are fading," Gallean growled. "Soon I will no longer be able to keep up the mist."

Caer threw her fist into the air. "Who's with me?"

"I am," the barmaid said.

"I am," the villagers shouted.

"And Gallean said they weren't warriors." Scott tousled her hair.

POOR PLANNING

*I*n hindsight I probably should have made the crescent moon garden larger, but then again, I didn't anticipate needing to use it as a landing strip for my two werewolf best friends plus myself as we jettisoned from Breas's prison to Granda's garden. I keep a firm grip on both of them when we land. I couldn't have them escaping now that they are in my clutches. One would flee to Clayone and the other to Breas.

"*Chruthaigh garrai gaghainn m'intinne féin,*" I chant as I rise from the garden. The ground and the herbs I planted empower me to retain my hold on both Ryan and Lizzie.

"*Chruthaigh garrai gaghainn m'intinne féin,*" I chant again. Invisible walls close in around them. I only need to step away for my containment spell to be complete.

"No," Lizzie wails, crashing to the ground. "You can't do this to me. You can't . . ."

I almost stop the spell to ask her why, but then, that must be what she wants—a trick to either kill me or stop me from imprisoning her.

"Chruthaigh garrai gaghainn m'intinne féin," I chant again, stepping out of the garden as I release them.

Ryan growls, trying to leap at me. An invisible force field knocks him on his ass. He tries again and again as Lizzie's wails fill the air.

I raise my hand, tempted to clamp her mouth shut to prevent her from alerting all of Ireland that I have imprisoned her. I cast a silencing spell on the cells instead.

"Ciúnas!"

Her screams quiet. Ryan's attempts to break out of his prison continue, but I can't hear his body smack against the sides either.

I watch them as I try to figure out what to do next.

My heart rockets into my throat as Maddie suddenly appears beside me and says, "Why are you standing in the garden staring at an empty space?"

I jump away from him. "Holy crap! How did you get here? Never mind. Whew," I say clutching my chest. I'm pretty sure I'm about to have a heart attack, but I don't think I should ask Maddie to call 911 given my guests—er, prisoners. Unlawful imprisonment is generally frowned upon.

Once I return to normal breathing, I smack him in the arm. "Maddie, you need to give me a warning or something before appearing out of thin air."

He drops his head and rounds his shoulders. "Sorry, I didn't mean to scare you. I'll leave."

"No, wait." I reach for him. "I don't want you to go. Tap me on the shoulder or maybe whisper in my ear, 'Hey, it's Maddie,' and then appear. But believe me, I want you here."

He smiles. "Okay. So, what are we supposed to be looking at?"

Suddenly on the other side of me, Granda appears. But unlike Maddie, he didn't appear out of thin air, he actually took the stone path from the cottage. Oh, the good old days when people took the old-fashioned bipedal approach rather than relying on invisibility and portals for their primary method of travel.

"Gigi," he says, crushing me to his chest. He's surprisingly strong for his old age. "Madigan told me you had returned but then became imprisoned by Breas. How did you get out?"

I look back and forth between them. Neither one of them has noticed the two people thrashing around in the middle of the crescent moon garden.

"Do you not see who I brought back with me? Ryan and Lizzie—my two best friends who I thought were dead."

Both squint their eyes as I point to Lizzie and Ryan's cells. Ryan is still trying to get out. He always was very determined and pigheaded, but eventually he'll come around. Lizzie, on the other hand, glares at me with pure contempt. It is going to take a lot more time to bring her around, especially after everything I discovered about her family tree.

When they still don't acknowledge seeing them, I realize I must have gone overboard and not only silenced them but cloaked them completely. I'm still getting used to my enhanced power.

"*Nocht*," I chant as I send energy toward their cells. The cloaking spell lifts, and now we can all clearly see and hear Ryan and Lizzie as they pound on the inside of their cells.

"Extraordinary," Granda whispers. "Albeit a bit cramped." His blue eyes twinkle with pride as he turns to me. "First, explain how you and Scott managed to disappear in the catacombs and where you went."

Ryan's growls intensify as he grows more and more frustrated at his inability to break out.

"Before you share your secrets, perhaps we should move inside, or you could place a noise-dampening spell on their cells," Clarissa says, appearing beside Granda. She also took the old-fashioned walking route, though I suspect that she possesses far more magic than she lets on.

"They're my friends."

Clarissa holds up a hand and closes her eyes. She breathes in and out—maybe scenting the air or having a vision, or performing some other magical trick I'm not familiar with yet. "They were your friends. They are now both working with people who want to kill you."

She did have a point.

"*Ciúnas,*" I whisper, returning their cells back to silence and invisibility.

Clarissa was right. If either one got away, I didn't want them blabbing about my goddess abilities to Breas, Clayone, or anyone else for that matter.

"Scott and I fell into a portal and landed in the Shadow Realm. I guess I can create portals sometimes."

Granda and Clarissa nod, neither one especially surprised by my portal-making ability. Tough crowd.

Maddie's eyes bug out of his head though. "Wow! Is that how you came back? Where's Scott?"

I grip my chest. Not on the cusp of another heart attack, but from finally acknowledging the emptiness of not having my brother with me.

"Still in the Shadow Realm. Caer ripped open a portal for me at Gallean's keep."

Again neither Clarissa nor Granda seems particularly impressed, but then, it was foretold that Scott and I would be separated for a while. I guess that's what the prophecy meant.

Clarissa's eyes shine as she reaches for my hand. "Gallean," she whispers, "how is he?"

"As disagreeable as ever. He finds our banter tiresome."

She smiles. "Go on."

"Wait," Granda says. "Who is Caer?"

Clarissa cups his hand in hers. "Caer Ibormeith. Scott's true love."

"Uh, excuse me. I find it offensive that she's only known as his true love. She's a kick-ass warrior who can rip open portals in Gallean's keep."

"Wait," she says. Energy fills the air around her. "She can create magic in his keep?"

"Well, if a portal is magic then, yes, she can."

Her eyes water as she drops to the bench beside her.

"What's wrong? No harm, some fowl."

Her eyes glaze over. Crap, a new fecking prophecy. I'm sick of this shit.

"When magic occurs from whence only shadows exist, the storm shall ring upon the border and crush its walls. The greatest of pressure delivers the truest of choices."

Crushing does not sound good.

Maddie crouches before her. "What does that mean?"

Her eyes return to the present. "It means the Shadow Realm boundary is failing, and it will no longer be a safe haven. The fall of the Land of Shadows will be the harbinger that the worlds are collapsing, and soon ours will be overrun with horrific Fomorian monsters."

"Including Balor," I whisper.

"Balor is dreadful. His fate is aligned with Caer, Scott's true love," Granda says.

I glare at him.

"Caer, powerful warrior."

"Much better."

"Why don't I think I'm going to like the sound of him," Maddie says.

"He is a one-eyed giant who turns people to stone with his gaze."

My stomach wrenches as I realize what Granda's words really mean—Scott is in danger.

"We have to get back there. If Caer's fate is tied with Balor's, Scott's fate is too."

"The real danger lies when the veils fall and the protective shields disappear. All the Fomorians will crawl back onto the Earth's surface. They will be able to return anytime they want to. They will not be tied to the moon or the rules of the universe."

"Does that include Fomorian witches?"

Clarissa's eyes pierce mine. "You've met one, haven't you."

"Well, not so much in person, per se, but one took up residence in my high school nemesis's body."

"She took a vessel . . ." Clarissa says to Granda.

"It's happening sooner than foretold."

I see you, the Witch scrapes into my mind, ripping off another fragment of my already questionable sanity.

As Clarissa and Granda continue to discuss the merits of different methods of preparation for the inevitable battle, I watch Lizzie and Ryan in their cells. They have both stopped fighting to get out, but I sense it is short-lived.

Of all the times for the world to come to an end, it had to be when I needed to provide don't-kill-Gigi therapy sessions to my two best friends.

Clarissa and Granda leave at sunrise to call a coven meeting and to collect herbs and other magical objects in preparation for the gathering. The topic? A plan of attack to ward off the monsters that go bump in the night.

Maddie stays with me to keep me company. His presence provides a constant source of comfort to me. It could be his connection to Alaric, or it might be because I am desperate for companionship. My best friends are locked in a cell across from me, vying for a chance to escape and possibly kill me. I've never felt so alone.

"How long are you planning to stand there and watch them?"

I fold into a cross-legged seated position, still staring at Ryan and Lizzie. "As long as it takes."

He sits down next to me. "For what?"

"Either for them to return to themselves and not want to kill me, or I figure out how to return them to themselves."

"Pre-werewolf?" he whispers.

I swallow the bile creeping up my throat. "Pre-werewolf."

"Is that even possible?"

"I don't know."

Evidently, when Clayone took the plunge into the deep end of the River of Blessing and changed into a werewolf, it meant that all future werewolves would have a trace of the River of Blessing flowing in their veins. Granda and Clarissa told me there was no way to remove it. Lucky for me. Heck, lucky for the world (and I mean that as sarcastically as possible).

But they don't know how desperate I am to save my friends. They don't know I would give my last breath to save them. They are werewolves because of me, because of who I am (well, at least Ryan is). I have to find a way to save them or die trying.

I open my palms to the universe and rest them on my knees. Maddie mirrors my position. His energy mingles with mine, creating an even more powerful force. Maddie possesses the magic of a werewolf, but he is also something else. In time I'll figure out what and help him control his gifts as Gallean and Clarissa taught me to control mine. For now, I'll make the most of his assistance. I breathe in and out, focusing on my breath. My sole objective is to find a cure for Lizzie and Ryan. I try to concentrate on the cure.

Cure. Cure, I chant in my head, but my mind wanders to Alaric and the time he showed me the Sacred Well of Brigit hidden in a thick grove of oak trees. Dense layers of ivy hung down from their branches, creating a heavy curtain from the outside world. A small babbling brook gurgled peacefully in the center. Wildflowers, herbs, and lilies blanketed the ground. Rays of sunlight shimmered down through the thick canopy, creating sparkles on everything they touched. The whispers of confessions were spoken in this grove, near my well. Alaric told me he had done terrible things. He worried that if we slept together, he'd become more obsessed with me than he already was. Only later did I understand just why we felt so connected. Cycles of our reincarnations, doppelgangers if you will, kept finding each other, falling in love, and getting ripped apart.

The second time I found Alaric at Brigit's Well, he was in a trance and speaking to a reflection in the water. A beautiful gray and white wolf stared up at me from the still water with intense green eyes. It was truth I saw there. Not an ugly twisted truth but a pure one.

"You," he whispered. "I knew it was you."

But he wasn't talking to me. He was talking to the reflection of me standing behind the wolf. He saw the shapeshifter nature of himself as a curse.

The werewolf curse tore us from each other in every reincarnation. Something tells me in my subconscious that this is our last try. A lone tear trails down my cheek and evaporates with the sun.

The werewolf curse is what started everything. Alaric begged for my help.

I am the answer.

If I could remove the River of Blessing and lift Derg's spell, I could cure every werewolf. I tap deeper into my subconscious. There, beneath the layers of reincarnations, comes the beginning . . .

A man covered in animal skin dropped a wolf hide in front of my other brother. Derg laughed, for he was not impressed. "A wolf? You want to become a wolf? What can a wolf do except eat a few sheep?" And on and on went his tirade until finally, the shaman spoke. "An immortal wolf, my lord. An immortal wolf that can change shape whenever he wants. Kill with one clench of his jaw. Destroy an entire village in one night. Panic and terror will rule the land, and your power will grow with every tragic death. I will bring you chaos. I will bring you destruction. I will bring you death if you grant me this one small request."

My brother stroked his beard. As a child, he never liked to share with Oegden or me, and he only grew more vain as the years passed. The shaman had appealed to his vanity and his thirst for power, for above all else, Derg wanted to be the most powerful god.

The shaman, with his purpose steadfast, entered the River of Blessing, drank from its waters, and survived. At the time, I worried about the ramifications of a man who could shift into a wolf, but Oegden and I stayed out of our brother's affairs as best we could. Little did any of us realize that Clayone intended to create an army of immortal werewolves, murderous beasts with the intention of taking over the world.

Later, Derg came to me outraged that a lowly shaman had duped him. While I felt little sympathy for my brother's bruised ego, I cared deeply for human life. I cast three spells to temper the werewolves . . .

Bound to the full moon.

Death by silver.

The herb nightlock to prevent the change.

As I come out of the meditation, I finger one of the nightlock-imbued crystals on my necklace. I never got the chance to give it to Alaric. Sadness combines with anger. As a goddess, I should have done better than alleviate the curse. I should have tried to remove it. I could remove it. Words form in my mind.

"Bain an mallacht a cheanglaíonn."

The crystal grows warm beneath my fingers.

"Bain an mallacht a cheanglaíonn."

Lizzie begins to wail as I continue chanting. Soon Ryan falls to the ground, clutching his stomach.

"Bain an mallacht a cheanglaíonn."

Maddie moans next to me. "What's happening?"

But I am too deep into the spell to answer him.

"Bain an mallacht a cheanglaíonn."

Blood seeps from Lizzie's eyes. I continue chanting.

"Bain an mallacht a cheanglaíonn."

Ryan screams. Blood streams from the corner of his eyes too.

A familiar presence emerges from the shadows.

"Bain an mallacht a cheanglaíonn."

Gigi, stop. Stop, you're killing yourself, Brigit screams in my head.

I continue chanting as Alaric appears in front of me, blood dripping from his eyes.

"Bain an mallacht a cheanglaíonn."

The blood-stained faces of wolves who walk on their hind legs surround me. I continue chanting, ignoring Brigit, ignoring the blood pouring out of the eyes of the three people I care about above all the wolves, ignoring their cries to stop.

I land on a cliff along the coast. In the distance, Scott

swings and beheads three creatures, only to have twelve more attack. His gaze falls on me, his eyes wild, battle fury taking over.

"Gi, get out."

Fighting erupts around me. I no longer know what's real and what's in my mind.

Swirling tornadoes.

The ground cracks and breaks apart.

Blood everywhere.

"When magic occurs from whence only shadows exist, the storm shall ring upon the border and crush its walls. The greatest of pressure delivers the truest of choices."

"Gigi, you will die here," Scott yells. His warning roars in my ears.

Gigi, you will die.

Alaric drops to his knees in front of me. "You're killing me."

My remaining energy seeps out of me, and I collapse in front of the crescent moon garden.

I gasp for breath, fighting to free myself from the tangle of objects smothering me to death. I kick and thrash. I yank and twist until strong arms pin me in place.

"Gigi, calm yourself," Clarissa whispers. "You're safe now. You're okay."

I wake to Maddie holding me down, with Clarissa and Granda hovering on either side of my bed. I wasn't getting smothered to death. My pillow and blankets got wrapped around my body.

"What happened?"

Maddie removes his hands and helps to unwind the sheets knotting around my legs.

"Well," Clarissa says, propping my head up with a pillow, "you have Madigan here to thank. He saved your life."

"What? How? The last thing I remember I was gripping the crystal."

Maddie kneels down beside me. "You started chanting a spell, and then . . ." he wipes his eyes. There's still a spot of blood at the corner of it.

"I made blood pour out of your eyes."

He nods. "Yeah, pretty much."

"But how did you break free?"

He casts a sheepish look in my direction. "I went invisible."

"And by going invisible . . ."

"The spell was lifted. Good thing, too, because you passed out."

"And that's when we happened upon you," Granda says.

The pieces begin to fall into place. Blood pouring from every werewolf's eyes, including—

I jerk up. "Alaric. Where's Alaric?"

"He's long gone," Clarissa whispers, stroking my hair back.

Panic seizes my throat. "Did I . . . did I kill him?"

Granda hands me a mug of tea. "No, dear, he disappeared after you knocked yourself unconscious."

Tears spring in my eyes. "He was coming to kill me, wasn't he."

Clarissa sits next to me on the bed, her presence like a powerful balm. "We don't know that for certain. He may have had other reasons for coming to the garden."

"To free Lizzie."

"Perhaps," she murmurs, stroking my hair. "We may never know for sure."

I sit up, suddenly remembering my vision. "Scott. Scott's in danger. I saw him in battle. I was on top of a cliff, along a shoreline, and he was fighting monsters." I gasp as realization hits me. "They were Fomorians, weren't they."

"Sounds like it," Granda says sadly. He and Clarissa share a long look.

Clarissa closes her eyes, searching her mind. "It's possible that what you saw has yet to occur."

"We need to find him. We need to help him."

Maddie rises from his seated position and gently pushes me back against the pillow. "Easy, Gigi," he says. "Easy."

Granda places his hand over mine. "If your vision of Scott battling the Fomorian army is real, the fight will soon be brought here."

"But first," Clarissa says, "we need to know what sort of spell you were working that almost killed you." Her crystal blue eyes try to penetrate into mine.

My head grows dull, my vision fuzzy around the edges. "You spelled me with the tea."

"Never mind that. We need to know what spell, Gigi."

"I was trying to remove the River of Blessing from their veins. I was trying to undo the curse of the werewolf."

She falls back against the bed.

Granda runs to her side. "Ris, what's wrong?"

"If Gigi had succeeded in her spell, she wouldn't have lifted the curse of the werewolf."

Maddie swings his head in her direction. "What would she have done?"

"Lifted all the spells she cast to bind the werewolf. Then the unbridled army of immortal werewolves would begin."

I hold the dull ache in my head, a reminder of the stunt I tried to pull. "Well, shit. That would have sucked."

Granda sits at the foot of the bed. "That is a gross understatement. What were you thinking? We told you that once the River of Blessing ran through a werewolf's veins, there was nothing that could remove it."

"I'm stubborn."

"And overconfident in your abilities," Clarissa adds.

I drop my head to my chest. "That's true too."

She lifts my chin, her gaze pinning me in place. "It's okay to be confident in your magic. In fact, it's the only way for most spells to be successful. But I would suggest for the immediate future that you check with Amorin or myself before trying a powerful spell. We don't want you dying on us." She winks.

She possesses a morbid, slightly perverse sense of humor. I like it.

"A good idea, but I probably won't end up doing it."

She grins at me. "Oh, I know. I was once young too."

"As was I," Granda says.

"I'm still young," Maddie adds, "and since I'm usually with Gigi, I'll make sure she checks with one of you first."

"Like a babysitter."

Maddie tilts his head at me, quirking his eyebrow. His eyes sparkle with humor. "More like a handler—to keep you out of trouble since Scott isn't here. And a bodyguard because it seems like you need one of those too. What with all the werewolves, gods, and Fomorian witches ready to either kidnap or kill you, you're in need of protection. Plus who knows what other monsters are about to surface."

"Nothing like a good pep talk to really get the spirit flowing!"

"Just keeping it real, Gigi. Just keeping it real."

Maddie might think that he'll be able to keep an eye on me, but he is surely mistaken. He doesn't know me as well as he thinks he does. He is only familiar with Ireland Gigi. I've been mostly on my best behavior throughout my stay. Vernal Falls Gigi is an unknown entity to everyone in this room. She's quite adept at breaking rules, slipping away without anyone knowing, and leaving behind a trail of chaos wherever she goes. My, how I've missed her.

"Now that Maddie's volunteered to be part of my protection detail, what about Scott's protection? There has to be something we can do to ensure his safety. Maybe cast a powerful spell to knock out the Fomorians?"

Granda squeezes my feet through the blanket. "Sadly, no. You are depleted, and if you tried to conduct any magic soon, and that includes portal creation, you could put your life at risk."

Here we go again. "I don't care about my life."

"And the lives of everyone you love, including all human life. Your magic could create a ripple effect that could kill everyone."

"Oh. When you put it that way . . ."

Clarissa pats my hand. "Have some faith in Scott. He's very gifted."

"A gifted pain in the ass."

"Gigi . . ."

The sleeping draught Granda slipped me was strong, but not strong enough. Not for a reincarnated goddess at least. I dropped my eyelids shut while the three of them watched me. I even made my chest rise and fall, pretending to fall into a deep sleep, but all the while, I willed the spells away until I felt them evaporate from my body.

They might believe that my magic needs time to recover before I conduct a big spell or else the world will end—talk about an over-exaggeration—but I've got some little spells in my fingers that'll get the job done.

I wait long into the night for their sounds of sleep. Maddie has taken up residence in Scott's room since his departure to the Shadow Realm, and Clarissa also decided to stay with us (code for keeping an eye on me). I chant quietly with my eyes closed. I don't need to slip each of them a sleeping draught—I can spell my own sleeping magic without the use of herbs.

When I'm sure they are all asleep, I crawl out of bed. A wave of nostalgia causes me to linger and take one last look around my room before murmuring a thank-you to the three sleeping beauties and climbing out the window.

Granda, Clarissa, and Maddie have no idea I'm saying my goodbyes to them. My new plan hinges on getting Alaric to realign himself with me. If he doesn't, the consequences will be pretty final, but in my heart I believe that our relationship goes beyond our current situation, that he'll break through any torture or mind manipulation or even spell to return to me. If I'm wrong, well, at least I tried.

Before I disappear into the night, I take one last glance at my home away from home, fully aware that it might be the last time I see it.

I remember the night Alaric snuck into my room. He was so confused as to how he got there, and I was so taken with him that I overlooked the underlying reason for his visit. His curse—for above all else, it is a curse—brought him to my room.

I stop in front of Ryan and Lizzie's invisible prisons. In sleep they both look so innocent and benign, as if no curse was laid upon them. Rage surges within me.

I will get my revenge. I thirst for it.

The dark countryside welcomes me as if we are old friends, and we are. It's been weeks since I wandered the wilds of Ireland on my own. A sense of exhilaration runs through me, even with the prospect of my possible impending doom. For too long I've been weighed down with responsibilities and drama. Tonight, I'm free—albeit for too short of a time because I arrive at the castle ruins much faster than I anticipated. My running along Ireland's hillsides along with my training at Gallean's, even if it was mostly energy dance moves, have conditioned my lungs to longer bouts of exercise. My Vernal Falls PE teacher, Mr. O, would be so proud.

I stare at the giant rock slab that imprisons Clayone. Bits of moss and grass have grown over the flat surface. Though I haven't been back to check on it since the eve of Samhain, it doesn't appear that the rock has been moved. Werewolves might have inhuman strength, but I doubt Lizzie or even Alaric would be able to move it. They would have to undo my sealing spell, and I'm the only one capable of that. The triskele carved in it would also prevent anyone from entering. How could anyone have gotten inside?

A pebble skitters across a rock behind me. I snap around and see nothing but darkness.

"Anyone there?"

No one answers. Big surprise.

"Maddie? Are you following me?"

Still nothing. Normally when I confront him, Maddie appears, or at least acknowledges that he's there. I study the shadows of the ruins, waiting for an attack from any one of my enemies, because it seems I have many. I whisper into my hand and send out a searching spell. When no one materializes, I let loose a breath I didn't realize I was holding.

I stare up at the night sky. The moon is in the waxing gibbous phase. In a few days it will be full. The Oak Moon on the winter solstice—a time of celestial power. The night the Fomorians would most likely make their move. I shudder at the thought of the Fomorian witch relinquishing Kensey's body for her own. I had witnessed what she'd done to Kensey's appearance. What hideous beast would she be in her true form?

The night Alaric and I wandered into the tunnels below Saint Brigit's Cathedral, I felt Lizzie's presence down there, and Alaric smelled her. Is it possible that there's another entrance to Brigit's shrine in the tunnel system? I'm going to find out.

OOPS! WRONG TURN

*B*efore entering the tunnel, I chant the spell Clarissa used to ensure nothing was lurking in the shadows of the tunnels. The ball of light shoots out of my palm and enters the tunnels on a search-and-report mission. Shortly after, it returns back to my palm undisturbed, solving the monsters-under-the-bed question.

I approach the tunnel entrance, but something stops me. A feeling in my gut—and the one thing I learned during dozens of counseling sessions back in Vernal Falls was to always listen to my gut. Rather than use a flashlight (which I didn't think to bring anyway), I conjure up a good old-fashioned fireball in order to see. Nerves knot my stomach and I have this shit show I call life to blame for it. Initially I was confident that Alaric's feelings for me would win out over any blood lust he might be harboring for me, but now, as I round the final bend before the large cavernous meeting cave, I'm not nearly so confident. Especially when a shadow emerges from the darkness and stalks toward me.

I'd recognize Alaric's body anywhere. His powerful muscles bulge from his arms and legs. It's been so long since

I've seen him that I want nothing more than to wrap my arms around him and smother him with kisses.

On impulse I step toward him. A growl ripples from his throat. A warning to tread carefully. But how can I? Through my many reincarnations we've always found each other. To be separated from him now after being apart for so long is a cruel torture that needs to be remedied.

I continue advancing toward him, ignoring the warnings trying to needle their way into my mind. His eyes flash yellow—another warning—but I'm drawn to him. I'm the moth to his flame. I couldn't resist even if I wanted to.

Step after step.

He bares his teeth, his canines protruding from his gums. A fierce growl riffles through the space, vicious and angry, and it finally sinks in that he wants to kill me. That in this reincarnation, at least for now, he's my enemy.

I stumble away from him, suddenly fearful that he might rip out my throat if I get too close. My first impulse is to run. My survival instinct warns me not to. If I run, the predator will appear, and any affection he might still harbor for me will disappear as his thirst for blood boils over. I slowly back away, completely unaware of my surroundings, only focused on him.

Kill, kill, kill, chants through my head, but the words are not my own. They belong to the man stalking toward me.

Panic bulges in my chest. My palms burn with magic, wanting nothing more than to create fireballs and lob them at Alaric. Granda once told me I was incapable of hurting another living being, but the heat in my hands is real. Maybe an immortal being doesn't count as a living, breathing human.

Magic circles around me. My protective instincts are strong in the presence of danger. I study Alaric's eyes for a trace of the man I fell for.

"Alaric, fight it."

My whispers snake through the air and circle his head. He tries to free himself from my word magic as he continues his approach.

I keep backing away. "Fight it, Alaric. Fight it for me."

He pauses, a flash of recognition appearing in those green eyes.

I smile, preparing to keep spelling him with words, but suddenly someone pins my arms behind my back. I try to break free, but it's no use.

In my next reincarnation, I better freaking come back as a body builder.

"I've wanted to do this for a very long time," a lilting Irish voice says.

I whip around, trying to catch a glimpse of my attacker. His yellow eyes roil my stomach.

"Declan, what are you doing here?"

He spits in my face. "Don't talk to me, filth."

Filth. Really. He couldn't come up with anything more creative.

"I know we never liked each other very much, but to call me, filth? It seems a bit much."

A swath of magic slaps over my mouth. "Silence," Maria/Carman shouts.

Were my visons of Lizzie and Clayone controlling Alaric wrong? Had Carman been pulling the strings all along? Could she cause false visions? Could she penetrate my mind? I know she's been three steps ahead of everyone the entire time, but I thought I'd leapt five steps ahead of her.

Maria/Carman prowls toward me, swinging her hips back and forth. "You might ask yourself why I took so long to show up. You figured out I wasn't poor mousy Maria all those weeks ago, but now, in this new form, I have needs and desires." She drags a clawed hand down Declan's chest. It rumbles as if he's purring. "I was waiting to build my strength and, in turn, my army. Declan."

Declan whips me around to face a tunnel full of minds I can't read. The minds of more werewolves than I can count. How had she been able to create so many?

"I am very convincing," she whispers in my ear.

My blood runs cold.

"But the one I really need in order to cause the level of destruction I'd like is locked in your shrine."

"I'd rather die than open his prison."

She flashes a wicked smile at me and a remnant of Carman's old face surfaces. "Oh, I know that, but unfortunately if you die, Clayone will be locked away forever."

"What do you want from me?" I growl.

"This," she says, taking my hand and jabbing a dagger into my palm. She throws my hand into the air. "*Chruthaigh garrai gaghainn . . .*" she chants, using my own blood and my own containment spell against me.

But who is she locking in? Me? Alaric? All of us?

She nods her head. Declan whips me back around. She throws my hand against the stone wall and finishes the spell, "*m'intinne féin.*"

"Enjoy," she says cheerfully as Declan throws me into the middle of the large cavern.

I sprint toward the tunnel that leads back to the Cathedral. If I can run fast enough, maybe I'll have enough time to call for Brigit's protection. My body slams into an invisible wall as I reach the entrance, knocking me backward.

Carman's cackles fill the cavern. "You can run, but you can't hide."

I lunge toward the tunnels leading to the dungeons. Maybe, just maybe, I can find an exit, or worst case, I could lock myself in a cell and try to call open a portal. I slam into another invisible barrier.

I whip around. Alaric stalks toward me, his eyes flashing yellow. I have to get away. Scanning wildly for another way out, I'm left with two choices. One is filled with Carman, Declan, and an army of werewolves thirsting for my blood. The other, an empty tunnel I've never been in.

Don't, Brigit warns me.

Alaric lunges. His claws slice my side as I leap away from him and crash into the rock wall. I scream as I sprint toward the tunnel, bracing myself for impact. But rather than getting thrown back again, I'm able to run right through it.

"Finally," a thunderous voice echoes through the tunnel.

I don't stop and overthink it. Besides, there's not much I can do about one little old Original Werewolf when I've got a hungry army of regular werewolves after me. I run as fast as my legs will take me. Unfortunately, I'm short so it doesn't do me much good. I never found this issue to be particularly problematic until today, though.

In the darkness ahead, a figure steps out of the shadows—a hulking beast of a man—and all my suspicions are confirmed. My sealing spell imprisoned him in Brigit's shrine room both above ground and underground, but it didn't prevent others from entering or exiting.

Imprisoned but not dead. The reality comes back to rip out my throat.

"So nice of you to join us," Clayone whispers.

If he didn't want to kill me, and I had a thing for psychopathic older men hell-bent on revenge, I'd think he was handsome. I can see where Alaric gets his good looks. With any luck he didn't also inherit his father's psychopathic tendencies.

With Clayone's massive form taking up the entire tunnel, I have three options. One, stop and wait for him to kill me.

Two, turn around and run back toward Alaric and hope that he has an instant change of heart (but even then, I'd still have to deal with the army of werewolves thirsting for my blood and the evil witch also hell-bent on revenge). Or, three, and to be honest I loathe this option above the first two, but it really is my only choice . . .

"You're welcome," Carman cackles in the distance. "Don't forget our agreement."

How wonderful it is that in her new form she has developed a sense of humor. However, I don't find it the least bit funny. She should really work on her comedic timing.

I suck in extra oxygen to prepare myself as I try to recall Dad's lesson from long ago. He had this naive idea that I could actually excel at a sport if I knew the proper technique. He was wrong, but his lesson stayed with me.

"Prepare to slide mentally," Dad had said.

Here goes.

"After you leave the base, run as fast as you can."

I sprint at Clayone.

Do you know what you're doing?

Now was not the time to layer in self-doubt.

Clayone spreads his legs and throws out his arms, but I don't think he intends to give me a welcome hug. Hot breath from behind me heats my neck. I'd be turned on if it wasn't for Alaric wanting to kill me. Godsdamn him and his werewolf speed.

"When you're close, throw your legs out in front of you."

Clayone's eyes widen, not fully believing that I am willingly running toward him. The element of surprise is finally on my side.

"Slide like you and the ground are one."

That was the part that always got dicey for me. The ground and I were actually besties, and because of that closeness, I always wound up tumbling or cartwheeling or eating dirt.

I kick my legs out in front of me and manage to slide between Clayone's legs. Once through, I leap up and make a mad dash toward the shrine room. I throw back my hand, murmuring a shield spell to block the entrance.

"Not fast enough," a voice drawls.

My stomach drops as I turn to face the frightening figure stalking toward me, his canines dripping with saliva.

"Alaric."

EIGHT OF PENTACLES

The dawn broke in a fiery blaze as the ground shook beneath them, but the villagers stood firmly in place behind Caer, Scott, and Gallean. They would die for Caer. Somehow she could sense that. Along the way she had developed a relationship with them without even knowing it.

It was like she'd known them her entire life. Sure, she had watched them from afar and snuck into their homes while they slept, but there was something more. Something kindred.

"Gallean, why are the villagers familiar to me?"

He looked away from her as he answered. "Because you've watched them since your arrival in the Shadow Realm."

Lie. Why would he lie to her? He often told partial truths, for her own protection he'd claimed, but he had never lied. As she became the warrior she was destined to be, she no longer needed the shelter of a child.

"There's something more to it. You're not telling me the truth. Why are they willing to die for me?"

His eyes softened. "When Balor killed your father and

took over the kingdom, many of his people were turned to stone. These villagers are the ones who managed to get away."

"But you said they were orphans and thieves," Scott said.

"Some resorted to thievery to survive, but they are all orphans. Orphaned from their land, from their kind, from their . . . queen."

"From their queen?" Caer's eyes misted. She couldn't be held responsible for their lives. She had one mission and that was to kill Balor at whatever cost. She couldn't worry about people she didn't know.

They're your people, Caer, a voice whispered in her head. It was the voice of her father.

"No," she hissed through gritted teeth. "I have no people."

Scott frowned at her. She ignored him. He may be her love in the Otherworld, but in this one they were strangers.

She gripped her sword. "I will kill Balor no matter what the cost."

The boundary shield shattered, and the heavy mist surrounding the island lifted. Before them, a mighty army of soldiers disembarked from boats at the water's edge. In the distance, tall ships with broad white sails bunched together, ready to be set free once their bounty was attained, to catch the wind and sail away from the Land of Shadows as swiftly as the winds could carry them.

She sensed Balor's presence long before she saw him. His very being sent a chill deep into her bones as she scanned the enemy. Soon her eyes landed on the giant. His hulking frame stood towering over the sea of beasts. His cold gray eye searched for her. His other may have been covered with a patch, but his seeing one promised pain, suffering, and death. She swallowed hard. Balor was much larger than she remembered, but then, she had only seen him through a small hole in the stone.

"Reveal yourself to me," he demanded to the small gathering of people around her.

It would be simple to merely disappear into the shadows. After all, she'd spent a lifetime hiding in them. But today she would not use her invisibility to hide from the beast. She stood tall, gripping Freagarach, and thrust her chest out. She would not cower before this monster. She would not falter for any man.

His gaze fell upon her. "You're mine," his voice rumbled through the valley.

"Caer, we're not ready for this fight," Scott said. "We are ill equipped. We aren't fully trained."

For a fleeting moment, she worried Scott was right. She was no more prepared to battle Balor than when she fought off the crocodiles in the King's washroom.

But she had survived that encounter. Thrived, in fact. She'd survive this one.

Balor lifted a silver sword. She recognized the handle as her father's. If his desired affect was self-doubt, he'd made a fatal mistake. Her father's sword fueled her rage.

"I was born to kill him," she growled. She refused to be swayed by such trivial concerns as training and preparation. Not with her father's murderer staring her down.

In addition to the legions of soldiers, mythical beasts also began to descend from the ships. Black hellhounds circled Balor, awaiting their master's command. They would be a challenge to kill, but not impossible. No one was impossible to kill, including Balor.

Gallean stiffened beside her. "There are too many. We cannot beat them."

She glared at Balor. "I don't need to beat them. I just need to kill him."

"Are you willing to sacrifice your people for your own vanity?" he roared at her.

"Yes."

"Are you willing to forsake Scott?"

She kept staring at Balor. "Yes."

"Even me?"

She almost faltered. Gallean was the closest thing to a father she'd had since losing her own. But she'd spent almost every waking and sleeping moment of her life with a singular focus: kill Balor. Nothing else mattered. No one else mattered. She gripped her sword handle.

"Yes," she growled through gritted teeth and sprinted toward the army.

She swung Freagarach in a high arc and removed three heads from their frames with ease. Blood splattered across her face. Her battle fury grew with each kill. Sprinting as fast as her legs could carry her, she raced toward her desired target. She would not be deterred.

The clash of swords beside her further filled her with purpose. Scott's sword, Moralltach, felled soldier after soldier. His speed, his strength, his sword were everywhere, clearing a wide path for her.

Kill, kill, kill, rang in her head. And she did. Dozens of them.

A loud roar and the gnash of teeth and claw filled her ears. Gallean had joined the fray.

"Charge," the villagers cried as they, too, surged into battle.

Caer ran and swung her sword, killing soldier after soldier. She found it was easy to take a life, especially one serving her enemy.

Balor stood in the distance, watching her. An army of soldiers and beasts still separated her from him. An army she'd have to kill in order to achieve her goal.

Balor voiced a single command. "Go."

His hellhounds lunged toward her. She had never killed

an animal unless she'd needed it to survive. Today she'd make an exception.

Balor grinned as he reached for his patch. If his eye fell upon Scott, Gallean, and her people, they'd all turn to stone. She would turn to stone. She cared little for her own life, but she did not foresee the death of her mentor or Scott. Or all her people.

Doubt etched her path. She lifted her sword. She had practiced launching it many times in the woods where she spent her youth and at the targets in Gallean's keep. Her accuracy depended on the distance. She was still too far. She doubted even magic could assist her. If she died and Balor lived, he'd take over the world once the veil was lifted. That couldn't happen.

She selfishly led her people to slaughter. All for her own ego.

A wicked smile slid across Balor's face. He thought himself victorious before the battle was even begun. He would soon discover otherwise. She raced toward him.

"Caer, this is madness!" Scott screamed. "There are too many."

"If I can get closer, I can kill him. The fight will end if I can reach him."

His hellhounds closed in on her. The stench of rot filled her nostrils. The hellhounds' last meal still clung to their teeth. She had but seconds before she'd be too occupied warding off their assault and miss her chance to kill Balor. She launched herself at a large oak tree and began to climb in order to avoid the hellhounds and to better position herself to get a good view of Balor. There weren't many branches, but she climbed it nonetheless. She squeezed and reached her way up the tree, using her sword and her boots to shimmy to the uppermost branches. The bark tore at her palms, but it did not matter. She had only one goal in mind.

"Do you think that tree will protect you from becoming my prey? My babies will push it over and devour you. Their hunger for your blood consumes them, and they will not stop until they are sated."

The tree shuddered as the beasts pushed and heaved against the bottom. Caer searched frantically for an escape, but there were no other trees close-by that were still standing. The onslaught of Balor's monstrous army left nothing but torn-off tree trunks. Loud shrieks of snapping wood rippled up the tree to her. She clung to a branch as she leaned toward the broken trunks and then leapt. As one foot landed, she leapt again and again, bounding from fallen tree to fallen tree toward Balor. She didn't hesitate. She didn't question how she was able to do it, she just leapt. The remnants of a final tree sat on a cliff far off in the distance. If she could reach it, she'd be well within range to launch her sword. She dove at the tree, soaring through the air like a bird. But instead of being scared or shifting into a swan, she felt lighter and more powerful than ever, as if she could fly for miles, as if she could fly forever.

Her people cheered and hooted for her. Their enthusiasm gave her courage. She continued to soar toward the cliff she'd selected for her chosen task. She was almost there when Balor roared, shattering her concentration. She dropped to the rocky shoreline, falling hard. The wind lashed against her, but nothing could stop her from achieving her goal. Not the elements. Not the monster. She searched for another tree or rock to climb. She needed height to ensure accuracy. After finding one, she climbed quickly and leapt for the cliff with Balor in her sights. It was an incredible distance that no man could reach, but she was no man. She was a powerful woman, and she would have her revenge.

He lifted his patch.

"No," Gallean the bear growled as he launched into the air over Balor's men. In mid-flight, he shifted back into the wizard and threw his hands toward Caer. A giant ball of energy shot from his palms as his body solidified to stone. As he fell to the rocky shore, his stone frame shattered into a million pieces.

"No!" Caer screamed. She raised her sword and charged.

An invisible shield knocked her backward. As she struggled to her feet, she watched Balor's army turn to stone in an outward wave away from Balor's murderous gaze. Any of his remaining soldiers within the shield were soon dispatched by Scott and the villagers.

Balor roared in fury and smashed his fists against the shield. The impact rattled her down to her bones, but the shield held under his assault.

"Mine. She's mine," he cried.

His desperation reminded her of her own hunger for revenge. Her desire to kill Balor had blinded her to the true implications of her actions. She collapsed to her knees. What had she done? Gallean had given his life for her. Why?

Love, a voice echoed in her head.

She cried as she banged her own fists against the shield—not to break through to get to Balor. No, to mourn for the loss of her mentor.

Scott wrapped his arms around her. "Caer, we need to get out of here. I don't know how long the shield will hold."

As if to prove his point, Balor wailed against it, and it rattled against the earth.

"We need to get your people to safety. Do you have enough energy left for a portal?"

She closed her eyes and imagined a gaping hole.

"Everyone, grab hands," Scott yelled to the villagers.

She felt bodies and hot breath as those remaining

gathered around her and Scott. In the distance, she heard the pounding of fist against shield.

"Together?" he whispered.

She nodded in answer, fearing her voice would be betray her.

"Together!" he yelled to the crowd around them, and together they stepped into the portal.

It was the last thing she remembered as the darkness took her.

Caer had fought gallantly. Not that he had ever been in battle formations before, but she had single-handedly killed upwards of a hundred of Balor's men on her own. He wasn't sure how many he had killed. Something had clicked in his brain when he saw Caer take off toward Balor, and he'd unleashed Moralltach. Together they were a formidable, unstoppable team.

Along with Gallean, they had managed to protect Caer and keep most of the villagers alive. He knew she hadn't meant to abandon them or him and Gallean in her desire to kill Balor. She had lived a lifetime consumed with a single purpose. When Balor appeared, something within Caer snapped. She couldn't be reasoned with or guilted into escaping. He and Gallean had both tried. The poor wizard had paid the ultimate tribute to Caer.

Gallean had loved Caer. Scott had often observed the wizard when Caer trained. His eyes shone with pride. Gallean had tried his best to keep Caer away from Balor until their training was done, but Caer was, in many ways, as stubborn and single-minded as his sister. After a lifetime of living with strong-willed women, he knew better than to trick himself into believing they could be dissuaded from their purpose unless they alone decided it.

He caressed Caer's cheek. She still hadn't awakened after she created the portal for the survivors. Between her fighting, her flying—he still couldn't believe that she flew without shifting into a swan—and her portal creation, she was depleted. She needed time to recover. He looked around at her people. They sat in clusters around the clearing, watching her.

A woman wearing black leather clothing with black spiked hair approached them. "How is our Queen?" she asked in hushed tones.

"Empty," he mouthed, fearing even a whisper would disrupt Caer's sleep.

"Let her rest, we will raise the shield."

Scott furrowed his brow. What magic did they possess?

She grinned at him. "In the Land of Shadows, we could not conduct magic, but here in our lands, our powers have been rekindled."

"What are you?" he mouthed. Caer was the reincarnated Goddess of Dreams, Sleep, and Prophecy. She was a shapeshifting swan and could create portals. She had even flown without shifting into the swan. What other powers did she and the rest of her people possess?

She winked at him. "Caer is our Faerie Queen."

"She's a faerie?"

"We are all faeries."

Gigi wasn't going to believe this.

14

IT WAS ALWAYS YOU

The look in Alaric's eyes can only be described as murderous. He desires to use his canines on my jugular above all else. There will be no necking, unless of course ripping out my throat counts.

My heart breaks. Doesn't he remember me at all? The love we shared—the lives we shared—all gone after weeks of torture. While I was in the Shadow Realm learning how to channel my magic, his memories of me were tortured out of him. The fact that he was able to leap into the shrine room before my spell blocked him demonstrates just how skilled I've become in my magic channeling (and I mean that in the most sarcastic way possible). Scott would say I let Alaric in on purpose because of some sadistic belief that I could turn him. He'd probably be right.

"You," he snarls, prowling toward me—and not in the sexy way he did when he took me into his arms in Devil's Den and began dancing with me. He now speaks in the voice of a man tortured until my name no longer brought warmth to his heart. Until my name had become synonymous with his enemy.

"Alaric," I whisper. "I know you."

"He knows that you betrayed his kind," daddy dearest howls from the entrance. "He knows you cursed the werewolf. He knows that—"

"Enough." I throw up my hand and toss a silencing spell at the entrance because, evidently, shield spells only keep someone from entering. They don't block senseless chatter from raving lunatics.

Now it's only Alaric and me.

Alaric's eyes flash yellow as he slowly approaches. There's no need for him to hurry now that there's nowhere for me to hide.

"Alaric, please," I whisper. "You know me."

I grip the crystals hanging from my necklace. His step falters as his gaze falls on them.

"I made this one for you," I say, holding one of them up. "It's imbued with nightlock to help ease the pain of the shift on the full moon. You don't have to change anymore. You don't have to turn into a monster."

His eyes flash yellow again. Shit. "Monster" might not have been the best word choice.

"It's you who's the monster."

Tears flow down my cheeks. I hate this inconvenient, emotionally weak human side to me.

It's the reason you are here.

He lunges at me. I fall back against the giant gold statue of Brigit. The very one he defaced in my vision. His chest heaves in and out. His eyes hold no recollection of what we shared. His claw slashes my neck, tearing the silver chain and sending the crystals flying across the room.

I gasp. Liquid trickles down my neck and I know it's blood. My blood.

His nostrils flare in and out as he takes in my scent. The

army of werewolves lusting for my blood awaits me in the giant cavern. Does he crave it too?

I'm about to find out. The next few seconds could be the difference between life and death, and I'd really like to live. But more than that, I need to make him understand what we mean to each other. I slowly lift my hands. He watches me cautiously but doesn't stop me. I rest them on his chest. Not in a defiant gesture or to push him away, but to touch him, to prove that I am not his enemy.

He stiffens, going completely still.

I just keep resting my hands on his warm, muscular chest and close my eyes. It's a risky move, but if I can channel my power, maybe I can make him see what we mean to each other.

I project the image of Metropol into his mind. The dance club in Pittsburgh, where we first danced together. The feel of my hands on him, and the way his hands felt on me. We moved as one being on the dance floor, knowing each other's moves like we had met a hundred times before. And maybe we had. At the time, I didn't know it was Alaric, but he knew me. He knew me.

He gasps and tries to smack my hands away, but I keep them firm against his chest.

"What was that?"

"A memory of us meeting for the first time. Do you remember?"

He blinks. His eyes flash green. He blinks again, and they return to yellow.

I create an image of myself at the football game. I'm dressed in a sexy plunging V neck along with a snug black leather jacket and black jeans. (I might have exaggerated the sexiness a bit, but I figure it can't hurt.) I stare through the chain link fence. I didn't see Alaric, but he was there watching me, longing for me even then.

He gasps again, jerking away from me. "Stop messing with my head," he growls. "Those are false memories. You are my enemy."

I step toward him, trying to return my palms to his chest. "I am not your enemy."

"But Lizzie said you were evil and that you must suffer. That I must cause you pain," he snarls.

He swipes his claws at my stomach and blood seeps out. I clutch my midsection, trying to staunch the bleeding. I might be a reincarnated goddess, but that doesn't mean I can't die.

"How could you?" I whisper as I slip off into unconsciousness.

#Gasping, I sit up and clutch my midsection. Alaric tried to kill me, or maybe he did kill me. I'm either still foggy or dead—I'm not sure which. I glance around and realize I'm in my bed at Granda's cottage, but I'm only more confused. How can that be? The last thing I remember was Alaric swiping his claws across my stomach in Brigit's shrine room.

Is this a dream? It must be . . . or maybe Alaric really did kill me, and I'm stuck somewhere in the in-between. I lift my shirt to inspect the gash on my stomach, the spot where Alaric swiped his claws.

"Bandages?" I murmur to myself. He really did try to kill me.

"What happened?" I ask aloud.

"He brought you here," Maddie says.

I glance over in the direction of his voice and make out his familiar shape in the rocking chair next to the bed. "Who did?" I whisper, not daring to even fathom that anything happening right now is real.

"I did," Alaric says, stepping out from the shadows on the far side of the room.

My heart stops. A giant lump lodges in my throat. I don't

know whether to be thrilled or terrified. I settle on getting to the truth instead. "You tried to kill me."

His face winces. "I did kill you."

But that must mean . . . "Am I dead?"

He's next to the bed in less than a heartbeat and reaches for my hand. Before he can take hold of it, I hide it under the blankets. He shakes his head sadly.

"You were until I brought you to your altar and begged for your life."

His voice is still scratchy from whatever torture Lizzie put him through.

"And what happened?"

I still don't know what to believe. Am I alive or dead? Gram and Mom didn't greet me at the door to death, the one to the Otherworld. Does that mean I'm in the Underworld instead? But then why is Maddie here? Maddie isn't evil. He's not capable of committing murder or anything so duplicitous as to warrant a personal meeting with Derg. Me, on the other hand? Well, human me was no angel.

Alaric reaches for my hand again, and this time I let him take it. After all, if I'm already dead, I may as well find some pleasure any way I can. His hand wraps around mine. An electric jolt zaps through my palm and up my arm, sending shock waves to my heart. Tears pour from my eyes.

"What does this mean? Is this some sick new method of torture?"

Maddie reaches for my leg and gently squeezes. "He saved your life. And the containment spell that trapped you in the tunnels were lifted when your life-force stopped."

I rest my eyes on the one steady influence in my life. "After he tried to kill me."

"Maddie, can you give us a few minutes alone?" Alaric whispers low and husky. Something just below my belly button awakens.

Maddie shifts around. "No can do, Alaric. My orders are to make sure no one hurts Gigi."

Alaric's green eyes flash in warning. "I am your alpha."

Maddie straightens. "You were my alpha. I have a new boss now."

My world breaks even farther apart. More tears fall. "Maddie, don't tell me you're working for Maria now?"

Maddie rolls his eyes. "Scott always said you could be thick. You," he says, resting his hand on my shoulder. "You are my new alpha, and I will do everything in my power to protect you, so stop sneaking off in the middle of the night."

"Gigi, please," Alaric whispers.

And although I know I shouldn't, the way he said please stirs something within me. More than anything I want to believe him.

I press my lips together.

"Please, Gi," he whispers, squeezing my hand again. Another jolt of electricity causes me to grant his wish.

"Maddie, could you give us a few minutes?"

"Gigi, are you sure?"

I stare into Alaric's green eyes, the very ones I've missed with all my heart for so many weeks.

"I'm sure. You can stand right outside the door."

"Amorin isn't going to be happy about this," he says, rising and crossing the room.

"I'm sure he's also not happy that Alaric's in my room in the first place."

"'Tis true. Fine, I'm right outside, but any noise, any cry for help, any strange change in temperature," he says, straightening to his full height and towering over Alaric, "I will take you down. I don't care if you were my alpha or my best friend. I will protect Gigi at all costs."

Alaric smiles at Maddie. It's a small one, but a smile

nonetheless. A flash of warmth melts another of my icy veins.

"I'd have it no other way."

Maddie opens the door. "Gigi, you need anything, you just let me know," he says and winks at me.

I will, I place into his head.

He smiles at me, nods at Alaric, then closes the door behind him. I can feel his energy signature right outside the door.

"I don't know how you won him over, but he is a formidable ally."

A spark of anger runs through me. "I didn't win him. We earned each other's trust when we were searching for you."

A pained look crosses his face. "May I?" he asks, gesturing to the bed.

"Since you've already tried to kill me—or did kill me—and I'm still here, I suppose it's okay."

He sits down next to me. His weight pulls my body toward him. Common sense tells me it's the Earth's gravity, but my heart tells me it's cosmic pull.

"About that . . ." he says.

But suddenly I don't care if he tried to kill me or did kill me. He's here. He's finally here, and that's all that matters.

"I saw Lizzie torturing you," I blurt out.

His eyes cloud over. "You saw?"

"I saw flashes of your torture. Every time you cried out for me, she hurt you."

He clenches his jaw. "I tried to fight it. For so long, I tried to fight it, but she broke me." He bends over with his head in his hands. His exhibition of weakness pulls my body from my pillow and causes me to wrap my arms around him. Initially he stiffens, and a part of my newfound hope dies, but then he reaches for me and draws me into his chest.

"What changed?" I whisper into the warm cocoon of his arms.

He breathes in my scent. "You."

Since the first time we met (well, officially anyway), he always inhaled. I didn't realize until I found out he was the son of Clayone, and therefore a werewolf, that he was smelling me. Now it's obvious. I'd been blind for so long.

"You still gutted me though."

He draws me in closer, careful not to hurt my stomach.

"When I swiped at your neck and your blood trickled down your throat, something triggered me, making me want to kill you and protect you. It was confusing, especially after the torture Lizzie put me through. The darkness in me fought against wanting to save you, but when I slashed your stomach, and your blood poured out mingling with your scent, something magical happened. I remembered everything. Every life we lived together. Every hurt, every death, but also every . . ." he pulls away from me and his gaze drops to my lips, "kiss."

I lick my lips. My inner Scott yells at me to stop, to not do it, but my oh my . . . I've longed for this man.

We fall into each other, and the world, or at least my world, sings.

LOVE IN A SECRET ROOM

*E*verything in my body screams at me to trust Alaric —that he is back on my side. Everything, that is, except for that pessimistic nature born from years of bullying and lies. That blemish, that freaking hairy mole, keeps needling at my brain to distrust him. That he's the son of Clayone. That he was tortured by Lizzie, his own flesh and blood, to hate me. How could I ever be able to trust him?

I take a shaky breath and break the kiss.

"What is it?" he murmurs, his eyes shining bright.

For once I embrace complete honesty.

"I don't know how to trust you. Your father spent fifteen hundred years plotting my death. You were raised by Carman who also spent fifteen hundred years plotting my death. You were tortured by my best friend, who's also your sister, until you hated me and wanted to kill me."

He stiffens. "She's my sister?"

"Clayone is her father too."

He shakes his head, gripping my hands to his chest. "It doesn't matter who my father is or who my sister is or who raised me, it's always been you, Gigi. In every life we've found each other. I saw that cottage along the shoreline. The tears shed as I swam away from you in the middle of the night to avoid killing you because I didn't know why I craved your blood almost more than my love for you. I saw the other lives we shared—all of them cut too short. We keep finding each other for a reason."

"What reason is that?"

He dips his head so we're a breath's width apart. "Love. It's always been about love."

I try to pull away. "Love? It seems like such a frivolous concept given all the torture and death you experienced in each lifetime."

He drops to the floor, kneeling in front of me. "Think about it. Why would I choose to reincarnate again and again after tragically dying each time?"

"Because you're a glutton for punishment?"

He smiles, his wolf eyes flashing. "I am a glutton for you."

I laugh. "That doesn't make any sense."

"Doesn't it?" He raises an eyebrow. "Why does Brigit keep reincarnating in human form?"

This conversation is getting nowhere. "To feel the emotions of humans. To remember what it's like to be human so she can protect them in the Otherworld."

He shakes his head. "No, that's the scripted answer. The textbook explanation. You keep coming back in order to find me. To find a way to keep me alive."

I snort. "Easier said than done, evidently. And if it really is the reason I keep reincarnating, why did I come back as a nun? A celibate nun." I raise my eyebrows for emphasis.

His eyes take on a mischievous, dangerous glint. "Because you tried to rewrite the story."

I roll my eyes and try to pull away. "That's ridiculous."

He won't let me free. Not without a fight. "You thought, if

you didn't fall in love, you couldn't be hurt, but you were alone."

"I wasn't alone. I had nineteen Sisters of the Gallicenial. You met Clarissa—she's a barrel of laughs."

"She might be loads of fun, but you didn't have me in that life. For some reason, we didn't find each other, or I wasn't there."

This line of thinking is dangerous. I might be many things as human Gigi Brennan and the reincarnated Goddess Brigit, but I wouldn't come back again and again for something so fragile, so fleeting as love.

"Listen, Alaric, maybe my visions were wrong. Maybe you're lying right now and only telling me what you want me to believe and not the truth—that you want to kill me because in each prior reincarnation you failed to do so."

"Gigi," he whispers, holding my face firmly in his hands, "Gi, you know it's the truth. You came here for love. You came here for me."

"Everything all right in here?" Maddie peeks in from the door. "Hey, get your hands off her." He rips Alaric away from me and tosses him across the room.

Alaric dives back in front of me, dropping to his knees. "Gigi, you know it's true."

Maddie pulls him away again and throws him in a headlock.

Tears fall from my eyes. I am a freaking hotbed of disaster.

Love. I came here for love? Brigit wouldn't be so foolish, so weakhearted as to risk her eternal life for something so fickle as love.

Love shreds you into pieces.

Loves messes with your head.

Love is the greatest emotion of all.

"Love," I whisper.

"What's that?" Maddie says, struggling to get Alaric out of the room.

Alaric spins out of his grasp and drops back to his knees in front of me. "Love."

"Love," I whisper, wrapping my hands around him.

"I'll give you two a few more minutes," Maddie says, his voice getting farther away.

"What is going on in here?" Granda says before shouting a separation spell that tosses Alaric against the wall. His arms and legs splay out wide, and he's pinned in place.

"Granda, it's fine. Alaric wasn't hurting me. He was just reminding me why I'm here."

Granda's eyes mist over. "Why are you here?"

"Love."

Granda clutches his chest and collapses. Alaric manages to catch him before he crashes to the floor and guides him over to a chair.

I stare in disbelief at the speed of a werewolf before coming to my senses and rushing over to Granda. His hands are ice cold.

"What's wrong? Is it your heart? Are you having a heart attack? Maddie call 911. Wait, do they even have 911 in Ireland? What's the number for emergency? It doesn't matter, just call it."

Panic much, Gi?

"Wait . . ." Granda pants. "Wait . . . I," he tries to catch his breath, "I'm not having a heart attack. Something is wrong with Clarissa."

"Clarissa? How do you know?"

He grips his chest again, wincing. "Our coven linked to each other after we discovered Carman was back."

Alaric stiffens. "Nan?" He glances at me. "Lizzie told me she was dead."

I hadn't had time to explain all the finer nuances of what transpired on Samhain before Alaric was kidnapped by Lizzie. And after what happened in the cavern, I'm not even sure what Carman's goals are anymore. Does she want me dead, or did she just want to use me to release Clayone? And what is the agreement between them that she'd mentioned? So many freaking questions, but with Clarissa in danger, there definitely isn't time now.

"I'll explain everything later, but first, Granda," I say, kneeling in front of him, "is Clarissa dying? And if you are linked and she dies, do you die?" Tears well up unbidden. With Scott in the Shadow Realm, Granda was the last link to family I had left.

"No," he pants. "It's not attached to our lifelines but our heartstrings."

Guess, I'm not the only family member who is a sucker for love.

His eyes widen. "Go to her immediately. The rest of the coven will be there shortly."

I shake my head. "I'm not going to leave you here by yourself."

"Maddie will assist me. You and Alaric must go now. There's not a moment to spare. Alaric," he says barely above a whisper.

Alaric shifts his attention back to him.

"I am entrusting you with my most precious gift. Take care of her."

Alaric's eyes flash to mine. "I will give my life to protect her."

"Carry her."

Alaric approaches me.

I back away from him. "I can walk."

"No," he says, lifting me and cradling me to his chest. "I'm faster."

Before I can argue, he dashes outside with me in his arms. Fear races through me. Will he turn into a werewolf? And if he does, will he forget about me?"

No, he answers in my head. "I will never forget about you again. I am just as fast as a man as I am as a wolf."

"How is that possible?"

"Gi, as much as I love you and want to relish having you in my arms, I need to get you to Clarissa's, and it's hard to concentrate with you asking so many questions."

"Do you know where she lives?"

He stops and inhales deeply. "Aye," he says and takes off into the night.

In the darkness of a moonless Irish countryside, I can't see a thing. I can only assume that Alaric's wolf senses also include night vision. Soon, he's rushing me up Clarissa's path, only setting me down when he gets to her front porch.

The door's slightly ajar.

"Wait," he says, ducking his head inside as he breathes in and out. "It's all clear."

Wolf senses certainly do come in handy.

I rush over to Clarissa's body sprawled out on the floor.

"Clarissa, what's wrong?"

She opens her eyes. Her pupils are dilated and rimmed with red. "Oh, child, something terrible has happened in the Shadow Realm."

My heart seizes. "What? How do you know?"

She clutches her chest. "I can feel it."

"Are your heartstrings connected with Gallean's as well?"

Her eyes water. "No. My lifeline. And something terrible has happened."

Panic grips me. Sure, I care about Gallean, the great wizard, but my brother is there too. "Is Scott okay?"

"I don't know," she says weakly. Her life-force is slipping out of her.

Clarissa has feared that bad things were happening in the Shadow Realm for a while, especially since Caer could create a portal in Gallean's keep, but I only thought the magical protective barriers were weakening, not that their lives were at stake. I would have gone when I first worried about Scott, but Clarissa and Granda talked me into staying. I shouldn't have listened to them.

"I'll make a portal right now and find out what's happening."

"No," she grabs my arm with surprising force. "It's too dangerous. If Balor is already there, he will kill you and everyone else he sets his gaze on."

"I'm not leaving them there to die. I'll open a portal now."

"No," she cries, refusing to relinquish my arm.

"What then? How else can I find out what's happening there?"

"A seomra de rúin."

"You are in no condition to conduct one on your own."

"She's not alone," Granda says, walking in with Maddie trailing behind him. Several more coven members appear behind him.

"Together we can combine forces for you to go and check."

Alaric whips his head around, taking in the scent of the new arrivals. Must be a wolf thing.

"What is a seomra de rúin?"

"It's an Irish room of secrets. Basically, I enter a deep meditative state where I can visit other realms."

"You're not going alone."

"No one can hurt me."

"Actually," Granda says, setting candles around the space we used last time, "you can't die, but you might wish for

147

death if the pain is severe enough and you can't find the key. It's possible to get stuck in a limbo space, especially if there is chaos in the seomra de rúin. Your only escape would be if the world collapses in on itself. But remember, time works much differently there. A minute here could be several hours there."

"No," I said. "No way. I'll find the key after I find out what's going on."

Alaric stops in front of me. "I'm going with you."

"No."

"I just got you back. I am not losing you."

"Possessive much?"

He clenches his jaw. He's in no mood for jokes. "Yes, I am."

I didn't know whether to find Alaric's need to not leave my side endearing or tiresome. Don't get me wrong, I missed him with all my heart, but I've always been something of a lone wolf myself (no pun intended), so to have him refuse to leave my side is a lot to take. The last time I went into a seomra de rúin, Scott was with me. We were making jokes about provolone and tomato sandwiches because we thought Clarissa was using salt to enclose us in the circle. Without my brother here, I don't want to rely on someone else, even if it is Alaric, but he strides into the circle and lays down beside me anyway. I hate admitting it, but I immediately feel calmer.

Clarissa, unable to gather the strength to create the circle, has allowed Anna, an understudy of hers, to spread the chalk and begin sealing us in with sage.

"Their energy signatures are very powerful," Anna says quietly to Clarissa.

"Don't worry. You have mastered the spell many times before. Do not overthink their origins."

I'm sure by "origins" she is referring to my reincarnated goddess-ness and Alaric's werewolf nature. Way to be subtle about it. Guess Anna doesn't have a lot of experience with supernatural freaks like us. At least she can cross it off her witchy bucket list.

Sam, another coven member, follows Granda's instructions to set up the four corners of the circle before Anna seals it. In the West, he places the bowl of crystals representing the Earth element; in the East, a sage bundle to represent Air; to the South, candles representing Fire; and in the North, a chalice filled with water representing Water.

I turn to Alaric. "You and I will serve as the fifth element, Spirit. And the gods know we've got a lot of spirit between us."

I'm still not sure if we're the type of spirits Clarissa and Granda had in mind, but I suppose we'll have to do.

The seomra de rúin takes a tremendous amount of magic. With Anna, Sam, and the rest of the coven members, along with Maddie, we should have all the magic we need without draining Clarissa and Granda completely.

I glance over at Maddie. He's kneeling at the edge of the chalk as if ready to leap across and save us—well, me—if anything goes awry.

"It's okay, Maddie. We'll be fine."

I know he can't hear me at this point, but he's studying me so closely he can read my lips. He nods, his eyes never leaving me.

Anna lifts her own athame and lays it across another sage bundle. She traces the bundle with the blade before placing it back down. She lights her sage bundle from one of the white candles strategically placed around the room. She holds it upright and Sam leans over with his own bundle and lights it, before dipping it into the cup Granda used the last time. Thin wisps of smoke begin to spiral in the air above them.

As the air fills with sage, candles, and some other incense, the coven begins to chant. Alaric reaches his hand over and grasps mine.

"Together?"

"Together."

16

THE DEVIL

aer's brain felt thick and fuzzy. Slowly she grew aware of her surroundings. Her head lay upon someone's lap. The hard bulging muscles hinted it wasn't a female who held her. She suspected she knew whose lap she was resting in and tried not to overthink it.

So she hadn't died or turned to stone. That was reassuring.

She tried to come to, but she felt so tired, so empty.

"Sleep," he murmured, stroking her cheek. "Sleep."

She attempted to pry her eyes open to take in her surroundings, but her eyelids were so heavy, and she was so vanquished. She vaguely wondered if Scott was spelling her, but it did not really concern her. She stopped fighting and gave in to the exhaustion.

Later, she became aware of someone tending to her wounds. Her gaze fell on a black-haired woman. It was the barmaid from the village, the one who had first recognized her. The woman hadn't been angry at Caer for killing the man who tried to attack her. Instead she had proclaimed her aid to Caer, Scott, and Gallean. Many of the other villagers had aligned with them as well. It was reassuring that the barmaid was still alive. Caer hoped that others had also survived. But Caer, after years of taking care of herself, didn't understand why the woman was still here, and perhaps more importantly, why was she taking care of her?

"What happened?"

The barmaid smiled at her and wiggled her fingers at Caer's head. "You brought us home. I am Keturah, and it is an honor to serve you."

Caer couldn't fully comprehend what "home" meant, or what Keturah meant when she said it was an honor to serve her. Exhaustion's long tendrils pulled her back under.

Some time later, she came to again. Fragments of ideas swirled around in her mind. She remembered fighting and bloodshed and the powerful warrior battling next to her, trying to keep her safe. Where was he?

"Scott," she mumbled, her tongue thick and swollen.

"Right here," he whispered, stroking her hair.

She stared up at him. He angled his head to stare down at her. His bright green eyes locked with hers. Just as she suspected, it was his lap her head rested on. His powerful muscles that were bulging beneath her. If the circumstances were different, she might be embarrassed, but with so much loss, her own awkwardness was unimportant.

"What happened?" she asked. She barely recognized the words coming out of her mouth. Her voice sounded garbled.

He stroked her hair off her face. "You saved us," he murmured.

She became aware of a sea of people surrounding them. They were the villagers from the Land of Shadows. The ones who had agreed to fight with them. After spending a lifetime alone, their energy signatures crowded her mind, but there was one she did not feel. She closed her eyes and searched for the wizard's presence, but she could not find it.

"Gallean?"

Scott's eyes shone with wetness as he shook his head.

Last she remembered, the mighty wizard was battling his way through the throngs of monsters. Balor cast a killing curse toward Caer by means of his stony glare beneath his patch. Gallean had leapt into the air and, rather than protect himself, he shot a spell at her, a protective shield to deflect Balor's gaze.

Gallean was the second person who had sacrificed his life to save her from the monster Balor rather than protect his own. She did not take his sacrifice lightly.

"The Queen needs her rest," Keturah said, draping a blanket over her.

"Where are we?" Caer whispered. Her throat scratched with dryness and raw ache.

Keturah patted her cheek. "We are back in our realm. Our magic is restored. Soon we will take back the castle and our lands."

A warning rang through Caer's mind. They were too exposed out in the open. They must hide if they wanted to remain safe from Balor's army. Caer tried to sit up. "We need to go. He'll find us."

Scott gently pulled her back down. "Your people created a shield to protect us. While we remain in it, no one will know of our presence."

Tears pricked Caer's eyes. "They'll find me. It was only in the Land of Shadows that I was truly safe."

"Hush, child," another woman said. "Have some faith in your people. You are cloaked in here."

Her people? The idea felt foreign to her. She'd never had her own people. Her father, of course, had his people. She supposed Mathair Mhór and Nimblefoot would have been considered her people, but they were long dead, killed by Balor's men. For years she had lived in the shadows without any people. Why then were the villagers labeled hers?

She lifted her chin to get Scott's attention. He bent down next to her lips. "Who are they really?"

He smiled at her. "They lived in your father's kingdom, and they consider you their queen."

She remembered now that Gallean had told her that when she'd asked him why the villagers were so ready to stand by her side.

She was queen of the swans, but Queen of Lake of the Dragon Mouth? It was a lot to take in. Her father's people had adored their generous king. She supposed it would only make sense that they felt the same loyalty to her, but she was by no means prepared to lead them.

She watched as the villagers bustled within the shield, readying themselves for battle. Caer once again tried to sit up, but Scott wouldn't let her.

"You don't understand. It's not safe for them. What happens when Balor shows up?"

Scott bent over and reached beneath the seat. "We will launch this into his eye," he said, withdrawing an iron spear.

"Where did you get that?"

"Keturah kept it hidden all these years."

Keturah stopped her shield spell work and looked over at them. "It was time to get it out and put it to use."

Caer slipped back into unconsciousness. Tiredness still plagued her, and she didn't understand why. She had killed many soldiers and hellhounds, but something else ate at her strength.

Grief, a voice whispered to her. She didn't hear the voice often, only when she slept sometimes, and even then, only as the faintest of whispers. In one word, she understood what she had lost. What the world had lost.

Gallean, the most powerful wizard in all the realms, had given his life to save her. He had lived for fifteen hundred years. Once known as Niall Gallean, the boy who sacrificed his life to Carman, an evil witch, and Clayone, the Original Werewolf. When Ris, the girl he gave his life to protect, returned from her delivery to Mathair Mhór, she bound her life-force to Niall Gallean's, thus ensuring his life for the remainder of hers.

Gallean had told Caer and Scott the rest of his story after he saw Caer reading *The Druid Sisters of the Gallicenial*. He had given up the name Niall and used only Gallean instead. Ris and Niall's magic had been powerful enough to bind themselves to each other, but after he trained her, that power threatened to overwhelm all the world if they remained together. Tragic as it was, they were forced to live separately. Gallean created the Land of Shadows, an island that was part of the Earthly Realm but hidden, protected by his powerful, impenetrable shield.

When Caer ripped open a portal in his keep, it should have been the first indication that Gallean's power was dissipating. That the Land of Shadows, or at least the mist, another safeguard of his, would disappear, allowing Balor to find Caer. She had never considered that Gallean would sacrifice his own life to save hers. But that was exactly what he had done. He'd allowed Balor to turn him to stone as he cast one last protective shield over Caer, Scott, and the remainder of her people.

And now, turned to stone and shattered into pieces, there was no way to reverse the magic and bring Gallean back to life. Rather than let the grief consume her, she grabbed hold of her thirst for vengeance instead. Balor would be hers. She gripped the iron spear as she slept. With it, she would ensure that Balor would not turn another person to stone, and she could live in a world without the monster.

She tried to read Balor's mind, or at least consider his strategy. Would he return quickly to the Faerie Realm at Lake of the Dragon Mouth to retrieve her, or would he continue to pillage and molest the uncorrupted, pristine lands of Gallean's Land of Shadows? Perhaps even take up residence in Gallean's keep. The very thought sickened her.

She opened her eyes to Scott's. He hadn't left her side since their arrival. She still didn't like the way her body reacted to the sight of him. Even his smell was alluring to her —a combination of sunshine and mint—but she pushed any betraying attraction away and focused on her anger. Her true singular focus.

"Do you think he will return here?"

"Who?" Scott asked, his eyebrows pinching together.

"Balor. Do you think Balor will return to the Faerie Realm?"

He breathed in and out. She couldn't tell if he was thinking about her question or if he was upset that she hadn't said thank you or asked how he was. But it didn't matter. Not in the grand scheme of things. She could clearly see that he was alive and unscathed without asking him about his emotional status. She needed an answer on her nemesis's whereabouts. That was the only thing that mattered.

"I don't know, but with the villagers returned to their rightful realm and their magic restored, maybe Balor won't risk it. He's lost the element of surprise he had the last time he took the kingdom."

Caer felt a mixture of relief and despair. It was her destiny to destroy Balor.

Scott lifted his hand to stroke her hair, thought better of it, and returned it to the bench. "According to Gallean's maps, the Land of Shadows is only a short trip to the mainland by boat. Balor and his men could destroy an entire population ill-prepared for him. The humans know nothing of Druids and magic or reincarnated gods, Fae, and werewolves. A few might be familiar with the myths and legends of the Fomorians, but they don't realize they are based on actual events in their history. They would be as helpless as your people were in the Land of Shadows when their magic was quelled and Balor attacked."

If what Scott said was true, the Land of Shadows would provide Balor and his armies the means to ferry over to the mainland of the Earthly Realm and restore Ireland to Fomorian rule. Scott spoke of hundreds, nay thousands of lives, more than she could even fathom, who would all perish if Balor's ships reached the shores of the mainland.

She stood up. "We have to be ready. We have to prepare for battle whether it's here or the Earthly Realm."

Keturah smiled at her. She unfolded sturdy wings from her back and beat them powerfully, lifting herself from the ground. "We will fight for you, Queen Caer. We are ready."

The ground shook beneath her feet. "Good, because it appears we are no longer alone."

17

17

CLEANUP IN AISLE TWO

*T*he warmth of Alaric's hand grounds me to the space. Together we'd visit the Shadow Realm and figure out what the feck was going on there.

Falling into the abyss of a deep meditative state is much less jarring than portal jumping. Thank the gods for that because I wouldn't want Alaric and my reunion to be marred by me puking on his shoes. I typically like to reserve that level of intimacy for at least the second or third date.

"Gigi, we're here," he whispers next to me.

I sigh. Part of me wants to stay in this dreamlike state with Alaric forever. No one is trying to separate us here, no one is trying to kill one or both of us, and we're actually together without anyone else. But the other part, dare I call it the more obnoxious aspect of my personality, is yelling at me to get my lazy ass up and find out what in the hell happened to the Shadow Realm and, more precisely, my brother.

Alaric pulls me to a standing position.

"You're much more focused in this *seomra de rúin* than I am," I say.

He smiles, his wolf eyes flashing. Since our reunion, the

wolf side of his nature comes out a lot more frequently. I still don't know if it's something that Alaric, Maddie, and the rest of the wolves could always do and they just didn't realize it, or if it has something to do with Brigit and her spell—the one I almost lifted. Yeah, it might have to do with that.

"It's not that I'm better than you in these new surroundings. It's that I don't want to lose any more time apart. I've been asleep. No, not asleep—living in a nightmare for far too long, and I don't want to miss any more time with you."

A weepy, sappier female would probably oooh and awww at Alaric's romantic statement, but I'm far too critical and more than a little callous. It's going to take a lot more than love proclamations to make this reincarnated goddess gush.

Okay, I might have purred, but I don't consider that sappy.

The first indication that all was not well in the Shadow Realm came with the silence.

"I wonder where Gallean is?"

"Who is he exactly?"

"Gallean. The greatest wizard of all time. This is his keep, and he guards against all intruders."

"We're in a dream state. Besides, I thought we were on the same side."

"Oh, he knows I'm on his side, but I figured his bear might want to challenge my wolf."

"He has a bear?"

"No," I laugh, pulling him over to the fire pit. "He's a shapeshifter. He adopted the bear to demonstrate his cranky side—though personally I tend to like animals better than people as a rule."

He shakes his head.

"Gallean?" I call out. My voice echoes through the keep. When no one comes or answers, I get a very bad feeling.

"Where is everyone?" I whisper out of the side of my mouth to Alaric—though I don't know why I'm whispering. No one appears to be here anyway. "Scott? Caer? Where are you? Come out, come out, wherever you are."

Alaric lifts his nose in the air and inhales. "No one's here."

No one?

He pulls me toward the tunnel. "I've got a faint trail. Let's follow it."

Nerves freeze me in place. "I don't know if we can leave the keep. What if we get caught in that limbo space Granda was talking about?"

He sidles up next to me. "We'd finally have some much-needed alone time."

Now, I'm overheated. "You do make a valid point."

The ground rumbles and the loud clash of swords fills the air.

"Hurry," he says, pulling me along like a chew toy.

I swallow the bile creeping up my throat. "What's happening here?" The outside edges of Gallean's keep waver as we approach. "I don't think we can go much farther. Everything looks like it's becoming unhinged."

He yanks me onto his back "Maybe we can outrun it."

I tighten my legs around his waist. "I don't think it works that way."

But the wavering edges of the seomra de rúin seem to pull and stretch as we move. He races toward the village, and there's one thing I need to get off my chest.

"Hey," I whisper in his ear, "don't get used to carrying me around all the time."

He growls, and for a moment, I think it's because I've turned him on.

"I smell blood. Hold on." He lunges forward, and I clutch my arms around his neck, careful not to strangle him.

We quickly cross the meadow where Scott and I first

landed upon our unexpected arrival in the Shadow Realm. We weren't supposed to arrive until the Shadow Moon, but whatever I did when I reached up to touch Alaric's image (okay, it was his ass) on the cave wall created a portal that took us to the border lands surrounding Gallean's keep. I tried a few times to recapture the intense emotion I was feeling to create a return portal, but I was unable to. Gallean had told me that no one could create portals in his keep, but then Caer sliced one open right in his freaking study. Guess the "all-powerful" wizard didn't know everything.

Alaric puts more and more distance between us and Gallean's keep. There should be at least three boundary shields to protect the keep, but as of yet, I haven't felt any of them. I haven't seen a hint of the energy of them either. It's like they're gone. At one time the shields were strong enough to keep me inside of them. A lump forms in my throat. Could it mean that Gallean is dead, or is his power simply waning?

Neither answer promises positive results. As much as I enjoyed the old wizard's company, I fear for the world even more. Gallean showed us the ancient maps and the way the Shadow Realm, the Land of Shadows, was beginning to appear on them. I pray that the fading of Gallean's magic isn't an indication of the thinning of the veils between the worlds, including the prisons and sanctuaries of our world.

Granda had told us about the Fomorians and Balor. What if they got out? Balor could turn people to stone with one deadly gaze. Caer was meant to kill him. What if she fails? Who else could be capable of killing him?

The ground rumbles as the boundaries of the seomra de rúin fade in and out.

"Alaric, we're going to get stuck in here."

"Just a little bit farther. The scent of blood fills the air. Something terrible is happening."

"There, in the distance," I point over his shoulder. A lone

female wielding a giant sword flies impossibly through the air and lands on a cliff overlooking the sea.

"Is that Caer?" I shout, squinting.

His pace falters. "Who's Caer?"

I tap on his back to pick up the pace. "I'll catch you up later, but she's on our side."

Along the shore, legions of monsters are fighting what look like humans. Helpless humans. My eyes prick with tears at the potential loss of all their lives. The fight is hardly fair.

Giant black dogs—hellhounds—leap at the cliff where Caer stands, trying to snap at her feet. She ignores them, her focus lasered on something else.

I follow her gaze.

"Balor," I whisper, half in awe, half in terror.

Scott and I had discussed the Fomorian in detail. Scott believed he'd be the size of the giants in Harry Potter. I scoffed at him, assuming Balor's size, like most things, was grossly exaggerated. A case of "mine is bigger than yours." We were both so very wrong. He towers over his legions of monsters as if they were tiny plastic animals he could demolish with one step. A giant leather patch covers one of his eyes.

"How can we ever defeat this monstrosity?"

A flurry of activity along the shoreline draws my attention away from Balor. A warrior moves through the beasts, felling dozens at a time. Blood spurts from headless bodies before they collapse into the water. He moves so blindingly fast it's almost impossible to track his movements except for the trail of dead bodies he's left behind.

"Who is that?" Alaric says with wonder.

I squint at the warrior. "Scott?"

"That's your brother?"

I smile as hope blooms within my chest. Maybe Balor can be defeated. I'm having a major proud-sister moment.

"It appears that Oegden, reincarnated God of Love, is a kick-ass warrior."

Three hellhounds pounce on Scott. He knocks them off with one massive strike, but more keep coming.

"They need help. They're never going to stop all of them," Alaric says.

I take off at a sprint. I might not be able to harm another living thing, but I doubt that Fomorians count.

Alaric easily catches up to me. "We aren't really here, remember? What can we do?"

"It doesn't matter. We can still fight. Scott and I battled with Gallean in the seomra de rúin. We need to help them."

The ground shakes with the intensity of the battle and we are thrown backward. Dazed, I lift up my head in time to see Gallean leap into the air as Balor slowly reaches for the patch over his eye.

"What's he doing? He'll get turned to stone."

Gallean shoots a shield out of his hands toward Caer. It encompasses her along with all the humans, including Scott. Balor's gaze strikes Gallean.

I gasp as Gallean turns to stone. His body falls to the rocks below and smashes into a million pieces.

Another blast sends us spiraling backward.

Alaric lunges for me. He catches me just as a roar, at least I think it's a roar but it's like nothing I've ever heard before, shoots us into the air. This has Granda's "limbo" thing written all over it. The ground gets farther and farther away before gravity takes over and we spiral down toward a small puddle.

Shit, this is how I'm going to die.

We grip each other close and slam into the freezing water. We never hit the bottom. We just keep falling and falling into the murky depths. We kick and thrash to get back to the surface, but rushing water keeps pushing us down and down.

If this is indeed limbo, it fucking sucks hairy monkey ass. I'm getting a refund on this ticket.

We continue to fall and fall, seemingly forever. At last, when I've almost lost the will to live, our heads break the surface. We gasp for air.

We finally catch our breath and clutch on to each other.

"We made it," I cry.

"We made it," Alaric agrees.

When my chest stops pounding like a herd of wild horses, I look around. Dozens of swans flock around us.

"What the . . . ?"

"Welcome to Lake of the Dragon Mouth," a woman with black spiked hair and wings—fucking wings—says, hovering just above the water.

"Lake of the who-de-whatey?"

A head pops out of the water next to me. "Lake of the Dragon Mouth, you spaz," Scott says, yanking me to his chest.

"Scott, I didn't recognize you without your glowing orb of Oegden."

"Shut up and hold on. I'll swim you to shore."

"Alaric?" I call out.

"Right here, Gi," he says, swimming up alongside us.

Scott tucks me under his arm, easily propelling us toward the shoreline where dozens of people (including Caer holding her sword and a giant freaking spear) are waiting for us.

"I never knew you were such a gifted swimmer," I say.

"You're dying to make a swan joke right now, aren't you."

"If the wing fits . . ."

His chest rises and falls as he laughs. "I missed you, sis."

"I missed you too. I see you and Caer are getting along swimmingly."

"Oh gods," he groans.

"Birds of a feather."

He tightens his grip on me. "Stick together."

THREE OF PENTACLES

"*D*id you know that I'm not really here?" Gigi said as Scott swam her real butt across Lake of the Dragon Mouth.

"You feel like you're here. You better not be starving yourself because you're depressed that you and I haven't been together. Your bones are jabbing into my side," he said, tugging her along to the shoreline where Caer and the rest of her people awaited.

She wriggled around as if to prove that, yes, she was in fact bony.

"Well, there were some complications back in Ireland, including our current situation."

"I would expect nothing less."

His sister possessed a strong bent toward theatrics. She would award herself an Oscar and an Emmy after what she believed were particularly riveting performances. Scott usually agreed with Judge Gigi's decision.

Moments ago, when the ground rumbled, Scott, Caer, and the people of the Faerie Realm, who had barely recovered from the last battle, were prepared to fight Balor and his armies again until their last dying breath. Then the sky split open, and Gigi and Alaric came tumbling down, landing in the middle of the lake.

"Alaric and I are in a seomra de rúin back in Kildare, though I think when that big fat stony-eyed dude roared, our seomra de rúin kicked into chaos mode and I somehow created a portal that got us here with you—wherever that is. Granda said sometimes it's possible to get stuck in a limbo space until the key is found, so I assume that's why we're here."

Scott shifted his gaze to her. "There aren't any keys lying around."

"Maybe it's a symbolic key. Maybe it doesn't always have to be a solid key."

"We definitely needed to find solid keys to get out of the last one. And remember how long it took you?"

"Here we go with another ego trip. I finally found it. And don't worry, I'll figure out a loophole."

He couldn't see Gigi roll her eyes, but he knew she did. He wished Caer could learn how to relax and enjoy life for a while like Gigi did rather than being so serious all the time. But then, Scott and Gigi hadn't had a one-eyed Fomorian monster after them their entire lives. It was only in the last few months that they had discovered werewolves, witches, and magic even existed.

He deposited her on the shore of the lake. "You always know how to make a splash. I will give you that."

She leaned over and retched half the lake onto the rocks. When she finished, she sat up and wiped her mouth with her sleeve. "Splash is right."

His sister was always classy.

When the spittle remnants were gone from her face, she looked up at him and said, "So says the guy who grew a million arms to strike down any enemy within reach."

He flopped on the shore next to her, careful to avoid her puke water. "What?"

"Alaric and I saw you fighting. Neither one of us believed it was you at first. You were always more politician than brawler."

"Ha! I'm not a politician. I just know how to use my words instead of my fists—or claws in your case," he said, picking up her curled hand, "or boots." He laughed, shaking his head. He couldn't believe he was finally reunited with Gigi after thinking about nothing else but getting back to her since she'd left. He had even been willing to go so far as to use Caer in order to return to his sister.

His gaze slid over to Caer now. She was sizing up Alaric. Scott supposed from a purely meat-and-potatoes standpoint Alaric was very handsome and strong. Jealousy flashed through him. Granted, he didn't know reincarnated Caer well enough to warrant possessive notions, but they were soulmates in the Otherworld. Maybe in their reincarnated forms, the rules of Otherworldly unions didn't apply. He certainly hadn't acted lovingly to her when he was hoping to use her to get to Gigi.

Thank the gods Alaric didn't encourage her by returning the attention. He hadn't taken his eyes off of Gigi, except for an initial passing glance at Caer when he waded onto the shore.

Caer walked over to Alaric. She inhaled deeply. "What are you?"

Alaric frowned at her then glanced at Gigi.

Gigi wrung out her shirt, unruffled by Caer's interest in Alaric. "Go ahead and tell her. I'm sure Scott blabbed all our secrets anyway."

Alaric straightened to his full height, his powerful arms and legs at the ready as a testament to his lupine strength. "I'm a werewolf, son of Clayone."

Caer blinked. "The Original Werewolf?"

"The one and only," Gigi added.

"I've learned much about him from a book I read, along with conversations with Scott, and Gallean." Her eyes watered. They still hadn't really discussed what had happened to the wizard, other than Caer asking where he was when she initially awoke.

Gigi reached for Scott. "We saw what happened. I'm so sorry."

"He gave his life for her," he said, nodding toward Caer.

Caer stiffened, gripping both her sword and the iron spear she had yet to let go of since Keturah had given it to her. "I will make sure Balor pays for all the lives he has taken."

Gigi cracked her knuckles. "I'm sure you will."

"But first," Caer said, redirecting her attention back to Alaric, "what are you?"

"I've already told you. I'm the son of the Original Werewolf, and therefore, a werewolf—though more powerful than most werewolves since I was born with the curse," Alaric said, before looking over at Gigi as if to ask, "Does she not understand English?"

Caer stepped closer, invading his personal space. Scott swallowed. He didn't like Caer anywhere near Alaric's lips, the very ones Gigi had once labeled "luscious slices of man-flesh."

Keturah and two other women closed in behind Alaric and inhaled. He shifted uncomfortably.

"I agree," Keturah said. "He is something else."

"Oh gods," Gigi said, pushing herself off the ground. "Please don't tell me he's another reincarnated god, because we've got too many of them already."

"No," Caer said, circling behind Alaric. Keturah and the two others rounded him with her. "He's part Fae."

Gigi wrinkled her nose. "Excuse me, did you just say Fae? As in fairies flying around spreading pixie dust?"

Scott grunted. Leave it to his sister to turn a startling discovery into a comedic interlude.

Gods, how he missed her.

Keturah fluttered her wings at Gigi. "Does it look like I spread glitter while I fly around?"

Gigi studied the wings closely until finally she lifted a hand. "May I?"

That surprised him. Normally she touched first and asked for forgiveness later.

"Sure," Keturah said. "Why not?"

Scott wondered if Caer had faerie wings too. He had watched her fly up to the cliff when she was trying to get to Balor, but she hadn't grown wings then. And when they had both shifted into swans, they obviously had wings, but they were the feathered variety. Keturah's wings looked like they were made of a dark, thick membrane like leather, but almost translucent. More like bat wings than bird wings. And there were lines that looked like veins running through them.

"Are those blood vessels?" he asked, pointing but being careful not to touch them.

"They are. Wings are a living part of us. Blood flows through them to make them strong and powerful."

Keturah's wings were black with purple and blue patches. The other two women's wings were orange with black patches. They reminded him of monarch butterflies. Gram's garden was always full of them. She kept an entire patch of milkweed for that very purpose. Could any of those monarchs back in Vernal Falls have been faeries?

Alaric slowly backed away from Caer and the other women. "I am not Fae. I don't have wings."

Keturah shrugged. "Not all of us do, but your mother

must have been Fae. Wait," she turned to the two other women, "do you remember Naisha?"

They nodded. "Could it be?"

"What?" Alaric asked, suddenly very interested in the conversation. "I never knew my mother or her name. She died in childbirth."

Keturah put her hands on her hips. "If your mother was Naisha, she didn't die giving birth to you. She was a powerful faerie, but she disappeared long ago. She . . ." Keturah's eyes brightened as she remembered something.

"What? Tell me," Alaric asked, desperate to know anything about his mother.

Scott recognized the hunger. Not so much in himself. He had been given a long history about his own mother growing up—none of it had turned out to be true, but still. No, it was Gigi who was always starving to find out more about her mother. She'd never fully given in to the notion that her mom was a "crack whore," as Kensey used to call her, although Gigi had made a lot of life choices based on that fabricated origin story.

"Naisha used to visit the different realms when the veil between them was thin. She talked about a tribe of people who worshipped wolves. She left one Midsummer's Eve at the Strawberry Moon. Let me think what the tribe was called. It was a very long time ago." She tapped the bridge of her nose with her finger.

Alaric swallowed, his cheeks ashen. "Was it the Diana Moon Cult?"

Keturah's eyes brightened. "Yes, that's it!"

Alaric stumbled backward as if struck. Gigi rushed over to him. Through the years Gigi had been called many things, and sometimes it was warranted, but above all else, she was loyal and protective of the ones she loved.

"Alaric, what is it?"

He turned to her. Her touch gave him courage to speak. "That was the name of my dad's tribe."

"What?" Gigi said, like she didn't believe him.

"The Diana Moon Cult was the name of my father's tribe."

The name triggered a flood of memories for Scott. "Gigi, remember the story I told about Clayone the night we went camping?"

"I've been trying to forget it ever since, but . . . what's your name?"

"Keturah."

"Keturah, you're saying that Alaric's mom might be alive?"

Keturah nodded. "We are immortal. It is highly possible."

Alaric pulled Gigi to him. "We have to go back. We have to find out if this is true. Nan said my mom died in childbirth. Gi, if my mom is alive, maybe she can convince my father to side with us."

Gigi blinked a few times as some realization hit her. "Wait, wait . . . Keturah, what did you say her name was?"

"Naisha."

Gigi paced around in a circle, talking to herself. "Naisha could be Nancy, I suppose."

Alaric stood in front of her. "Nancy? Who's Nancy?"

Gigi swallowed. "Lizzie's mom."

Alaric's eyes flashed gold, and Scott saw the wolf he was.

"We need to go," Alaric said.

Scott didn't understand what all the fuss was about. Why did Gigi think Lizzie's mom could be Alaric's mom?

Because Lizzie's dad is Clayone, Gigi dropped in his head.

What the . . . ? It was Scott's turn to stumble backward in shock.

Before he could ask more, Alaric and Gigi grabbed each other's hands and disappeared.

Gigi and Alaric disappeared in front of their eyes. Caer did not sense magic from a portal, nor did she see an opening in the universe—both indications that a portal was used. What then?

"Where did they go? How did that happen?"

Scott stared at the place where Gigi and Alaric had vanished. "Gigi said they visited the Land of Shadows through a seomra de rúin, a room of secrets one can visit in a deep meditative state, but a tremendous amount of magic is required to conduct it."

"And your realm has powerful witches and wizards capable of conducting such magic?"

She remembered when Scott and Gigi had visited Gallean through a seomra de rúin prior to their arrival for training. And there were others who had sought him throughout the years by such means. She hadn't realized it was a powerful magic though. That would explain why Gallean was surprised she had been able to penetrate it. It must also mean that she possessed her own type of powerful magic beyond that of portal making and invisibility. But after baring her soul so much during her time with Scott and losing Gallean today, she was not prepared to explore the boundaries of her own magic at the present. Someday, perhaps when she was alone, she'd examine, but not in front of so many witnesses. Yes, they were her people, but mostly they were strangers with only a passing familiarity.

Scott studied her for an uncomfortably long time. She shifted her feet. The motion snapped him out of his trance.

"Clarissa is a very powerful witch. You might know her as Ris from that book you were reading. My granda is also a powerful Druid, our name for wizard."

Caer found it incredible that all the characters from what she had originally thought was just a story still lived today.

Or did live until today. Sadness filled her. But there were still many unanswered questions.

"Are there others capable of conducting this magic?"

"There are other members of their coven, a Druid circle actually, though they call it a coven. Anyway, there are others who have experience with magic, but I don't know if they're capable of conducting that high a level of magic. Why?"

"Gallean told us his life-force was connected with Clarissa's."

He stumbled backward. "I hadn't thought of that. Gigi assumed they were stuck in a kind of limbo after the battle, and that's how they were able to come here."

Then it hit her. She threw out her arms with excitement, careful not to hit anyone with her sword or her spear. "When they landed in the lake, they came through a portal. Is it possible to create a portal in a seomra de rúin?"

"I guess, but the magic required . . ." Scott began circling the perimeter, scratching his head. He had not slipped into god-speed yet, but it looked like he was trying to work out a number of different things. Suddenly he stopped. "All the magic you can do, all the magic Gigi can do—everyone said none of that magic could be done, but yet, you both were able to create portals at different unexpected times. You were able to create a portal in Gallean's keep. Gigi created one in the seomra de rúin. Along with the fact that Balor's armies were able to break through Gallean's boundaries, even if Gallean's magic was weakening . . . the magic seems wonky— like it's malfunctioning and amplifying at the same time."

Caer appreciated that Scott explained what "wonky" meant.

"So what should we do? Should we go into our own seomra de rúin to find out what's going on? Do we travel through a portal in case Balor arrives on the mainland of your realm? Do we take possession of the castle? What action do we take?"

"I don't know." He collapsed to the ground. The earth vibrated through her.

"Wait," he said, pushing himself up. "We could meditate. We might be able to find out answers then."

"Meditate?" she whispered. The last time she had mediated with Scott and Gallean, she had fantasized about Scott as a warrior and all the things he could do with her body. She really didn't want to reignite the fire she had recently done a fairly good job of dousing. "No, there has to be another way."

"Caer," he said, reaching for the hand that held Freagarach before she had a chance to pull it away. He returned the sword to its scabbard. "It's our best chance of figuring out what we should do next."

"But . . ."

She tried to pull away from him, but he held her firmly.

"I'll be right with you. I won't let anything happen to you."

She swallowed, trying hard not to stare at his lips and trying even harder not to lick hers. She hoped that he was right, and she hoped even more that she could keep her hands off of him in their meditative state. After all, she had a kingdom to rule, a Fomorian monster to kill, and her people to protect. She couldn't let the vibrations of desire that rippled through her body take control. She was stronger than that. Was she not?

QUEEN OF SWORDS

*T*he crystal throne sparkled before her, tempting her, taunting her to take her rightful place as Queen of the Faerie Realm. She had never dreamt of ruling a kingdom. After Balor had sliced her father's throat in front of her, she had run. Through the many years since his death, running had ruled her. She had run from the monster who killed her father for fear of getting her own throat slit. She had run from the village children in the marketplace when they thought her a monster after she surfaced from the river. She had run from the Lovers card Mathair Mhór had pulled the night of her death. She had run from the pain of losing the one woman who had taken her in and cared for her as if she were her own flesh and blood. She had run from Gallean's keep in anger when he cast her away. She'd been running from her own monster her entire life. It was only when she had returned to her father's kingdom at Lake of the Dragon Mouth that she embraced her inner monster, her swan.

Now the crystal throne called to her. The ancient faerie music of the harp sang to her, vibrating in her bones, in her soul. It knew she was close and wanted her to reclaim it. To place the crown upon her head and take her seat as Queen of the Lake of the Dragon Mouth Kingdom.

The thrill of anticipation rushed through her. The throne was almost hers. A part of her believed if she could just sit upon it, she'd discover the means to defeat Balor. The iron spear was the tool she'd use to take him down, but she did not know the method. How was she to get close enough to pierce his open eye without turning to stone herself?

Gallean had given his life to protect her. She must discover the means by which to kill Balor before warring against him in battle and endangering the lives of all those who would stand by her side. She must find a way to destabilize his power, if only for a heartbeat, before she launched the spear into his eye.

Legends suggested a man would kill Balor. The old legends were wrong. A man would purely send Balor along with the rest of the Fomorians to a black purgatory in the Otherworld for all his evils, but that location was not his permanent destination. Balor's true fate fell to a woman's hand, to Caer's, and she would fill the promise brilliantly. The only question was, how?

She stalked in front of the crystal throne. Even during her periods of reflection, she couldn't bring herself to sit upon her father's throne. Perhaps she'd wait until she was rid of Balor for good. But when would that be? She did not know. She had so many questions and so few answers.

Patience child, Mathair Mhór thrummed through her mind.

The surprise of hearing the old woman's voice almost broke her out of the meditation. Mathair Mhór had never communicated with her during all her time of solitude in the cave. Not even when she was at her weakest physically and emotionally from lack of food and companionship did the old woman's spirit visit, but now, with Scott and her people nearby, Mathair Mhór appeared.

Why now? Why when the crystal throne tempted Caer to claim her title? Why couldn't the old woman have come when she was starving? Almost dying from eating the rotten rabbit? Why hadn't she come then to help heal her? Why now?

Your throne can wait. Your people will safeguard it. You are needed elsewhere.

Where else was more important than taking her throne and killing Balor? It was her destiny. Mathair Mhór herself had told her that.

Your destiny is entwined with your Lover's, and he is needed elsewhere.

Fire ignited before him. His sister was in great danger. The meditation brought that sense of warning rushing to the surface. So immediate, it burned his skin.

He kicked and pulled at the fog, trying to reach the surface and break out of the meditation. The fog kept pushing him down, fighting to keep him under. Gigi needed him, but even more than that, he felt the world needed him. Like soon they'd be under attack, and there'd be nothing left of the Earthly Realm but a broken, burnt-out shell.

He thrashed. He kicked. He'd break out of this fog if it was the last thing he ever did. He roared in frustration. It was enough to bring him out of the fog.

His eyes snapped open. He needed to get to Gigi now.

Caer lay beside him, her eyes pulsing beneath her lids as she journeyed through her own meditation. She looked so peaceful in her stillness. He didn't want to abruptly awaken her, but Gigi's life was at stake, and Caer was the only one who could send him back to the Earthly Realm. He loathed having to leave her alone in the Faerie Realm with the possibility that Balor could appear at any moment, but she had her people, and they had their magic now. They could protect her. They had proven lethal and ferocious even without their magic, and now, fully restored to their former selves, they could guard.

Scott would come back to Caer once every threat to Gigi was eliminated. He had killed many at the Battle of the Land of Shadows. He would strike down anyone who dared to harm his sister.

"Caer," he said, gently shaking her. "Caer, wake up."

She slowly blinked her eyes open. She must have gone very deep into the meditation.

"Caer, I need your help."

She tensed. "What is it?"

"Gigi is under attack, and I need to protect her."

She leapt to her feet in an athletic move that would make Olympic gymnasts envious. She was a power to behold.

"Well, let's go."

"No," he said, slowly approaching her. She had a tendency to swing her sword around whenever the mood hit her, and the mood struck her often. "You need to stay. You need to be with your people. To . . . protect them."

Surprise flashed across her features until the fierce warrior returned. "You're leaving me?"

Oh gods, she was beautiful.

He sensed the sadness in her and the taste of betrayal.

"I will return. I just need to protect Gigi, and then I'll return to you."

"How? How will you return?"

"I'll have Gigi make a portal?"

"You told me that all magic is wonky right now, and her portal creation is already not as consistent as mine."

What she said was true, but he'd do everything in his power to get back to her.

"I will come back to you. I promise. I will not leave you alone and unprotected from Balor, but I need to hurry. Will you make me one? Please?"

Her eyes softened. She warred with herself. She set her jaw. "No, I'm going with you. Two warriors are better than one."

Caer, above all else, was a warrior. He would be hard-pressed to find her equal, but he couldn't ask her to leave her kingdom to help his sister so quickly after arriving.

"What about your people?"

"Keturah," she called over her shoulder.

Keturah rushed over, bowing before her. "Yes, Your Majesty."

"You are in change until I return."

With her head still bent, she said, "It would be my greatest honor."

"Keturah," Caer whispered, "you don't need to bow or kneel before me."

Keturah lifted her chin. "It is an honor we bestow upon our leader, and you are our Queen."

"Thank you," she nodded before turning back to him. "Let's go."

"Wait, take this," Keturah said, handing her the iron spear, which had lain by her side during her meditation. "Just in case you need it."

Caer took the spear and raised her sword, preparing to slice open a portal.

"Wait," Keturah shouted. "Take this too," she said, handing her a small mirror. "Call for me through this. We will come to your aid."

Scott didn't know how Keturah and the rest of them could travel to the Earthly Realm without a portal. Maybe they'd fly there? But he didn't have time to stick around and ask questions. He had a sister to save.

"Let's do this," Caer said, swinging Freagarach in a wide arc to rip open the portal. She took his hand in hers, and they leapt through.

CAN YOU CLONE ME NOW?

*A*laric and I gasp for breath as we sit up. Suffocating heat stifles any chance of getting oxygen into our lungs, and by the gods we need oxygen after nearly drowning again as we got yanked through limbo a second time.

But evidently breathing would have to wait because our arrival back in the Earthly Realm is marked by fire. Outside the chalk circle, flames devour Clarissa's living room. The curtains, the sofa, the rug, the books—all of it.

"What the fuck's happening?" I scream.

But no one answers, which, given the height of the flames and the efforts Anna, Sam, and the rest of the coven members are putting into dousing the fire, makes sense. Then I remember no one can hear us outside the circle, which normally wouldn't be an issue, but since they're all involved in firefighting, no one can break the circle for us either. We're bound in until the chalk line is broken.

Anna uses a wool blanket to stop the fire from reaching Clarissa's slumped-over frame. Sam wields the world's largest fire extinguisher and shoots it at the curtains as the flames curl up to the ceiling. A few other coven members are taking similar actions to no effect. Nothing will stop the fire.

"It's not natural," I say to myself.

"Can you stop it? Gigi, you have to stop it." Alaric tries to get out of the circle, but he can't pass the chalk line. Magic is still keeping us locked within.

But here's the thing: I am a fucking reincarnated goddess. If I can't break a thin line of chalk, the worlds are in big trouble.

I chant as I throw out my hands. Energy explodes out of them, breaks the chalk line, and skims the fire. I fold my fingers into my palms and the flames get sucked into them like a vacuum.

My chest heaves from the effort, but there's no time to recover. Ash chunks start falling to the floor. The walls sway back and forth, creaking and moaning. The place is going to collapse any second.

I scan the room for Clarissa and Granda. Clarissa's still slumped over in her rocking chair. Anna's trying to do a healing spell, but she doesn't know what I know. Clarissa and Gallean's lifelines were linked, and now that he's dead, her death is inevitable. Tears prick my eyes. I blink them away. There's no time for emotional breakdowns. Not when we've got to get everyone out before they're crushed to death.

I haven't found Granda yet. Panic grips me. Where is he? My eyes search the room frantically. In the far corner, I see Maddie's giant frame bent over someone.

"Granda!"

"Here, child," he says weakly from behind one of my new favorite people.

Maddie helps him off the floor. "I got him."

Granda's life-force is severely weakened. The old man's not going to die if I have anything to say about it.

"Maddie, what the fuck happened?"

183

He shakes his head. He doesn't know any more than the rest of them, and Granda is in no condition to speak. Besides, we don't have time for a hug-it-out session right now, and I have a feeling I know who's behind this anyway.

"Take him outside," I order him.

He hesitates at the door. "Do you think it's safe?"

Gallean taught me many things in the Shadow Realm, and now I wield power befitting a goddess. I throw a protective shield over the entire property.

"It is now."

Maddie quickly takes Granda outside. Sam follows closely behind, whispering a strong healing spell. Good. Granda needs all the healing he can get. He's in capable hands until I can get to him.

The floor shakes, and another chunk of the ceiling falls. Any minute now the entire house will collapse.

Anna's still tending to Clarissa.

"Alaric, help Anna get Clarissa outside. It isn't safe in here."

"I'm not leaving you," he says, picking up Clarissa's still frame.

"Go."

He hesitates.

"Now." I throw an energy ball at him that pushes them out the door.

"The rest of you, leave now," I roar as I rip some of Clarissa's spell books off the shelf, grab a bowl of crystals, and head for the door. I take one last glance around to make sure I've grabbed everything I need.

Clarissa's spirit floats above the floor. She hands me her athame. *Protect them.*

"Always."

She nods, fading away to nothingness.

I step over the threshold as the roof collapses.

I turn around and stare at the remainder of the coven. Most are sitting on the ground, coughing, trying to catch their breath. But breathing doesn't matter, not if Breas and Fomorian Witch Kensey are somewhere nearby preparing to kill us.

I send my mind outside the shield. Faintly, I sense their slippery, gloating presence.

Got you, Witch Kensey says, scraping against my mind.

She just can't resist signaling her presence, along with the arrival of more of her minions. Thankfully the element of surprise is beyond her grasp.

"It was a trap," I say to no one in particular. "*Incendio*," I shout, throwing up a ring of fire to protect us from the encroaching enemy, because my boundary spell may not be strong enough to keep them out.

"Gigi, how do we get away now? We've no place to go," Anna cries, shielding Clarissa's body from the flames.

I bend down and touch her shoulder. Her brown eyes are wary. I may be a reincarnated goddess, but she doesn't trust me entirely. Not after I've caused so much destruction and death. "Anna, Clarissa is no longer with us. Her life-force was tied to the great wizard, Gallean. He died at the hands of Balor."

"The Fomorian of legend? The one who turns people to stone?" she cries, her voice tinged with wonder and disbelief that the legend of Balor is real.

"Yes, sadly."

She begins to shake in panic.

I grip her shoulder and push soothing magic into her. "But we still have work to do. Amorin needs you. I need you."

Her eyes focus on mine. I didn't mean to word-spell her, but I think I might have.

"You take care of Amorin," I say. "I'll take care of everything else."

She nods, says a few words to Clarissa's body, and crawls over to Granda.

Alaric touches my arm. "You're not taking care of everything on your own."

My heart fills with warmth. Resolve blooms within me, as does my authority. Protecting my people is what I was born to do.

"You guard everyone within the circle."

"What are you going to do?"

"I'm going to see if my magic can disable a Fomorian witch who's inhabiting my high school nemesis, along with a god who thinks he's my husband."

Alaric growls. His protective side rages next to me. Evidently he really dislikes anyone else trying to claim me. His emotion makes my magic more powerful.

"And if you can't?"

Maddie hurries over. His heightened werewolf senses allow him to hear over the din of the flames. "You know you can't hurt another living thing. Clarissa and Amorin both told you that." The fear in his eyes is unmistakable.

"Then I'll open a portal and we'll disappear. We can go to Scott and Caer."

Alaric pulls me to him. "No, that will lead everyone to that realm. They could destroy all of us in one swift move. Besides, it's not their realm the Fomorian's want, it's this one."

Tick tock, Witch Kensey hisses.

Anger fills me. They will not win. Not today. Not ever.

"You've got that right, sis," Scott says, appearing beside me.

"My sword thirsts for blood," Caer says, crouching into a fighting position.

"You are one scary-ass bitch, you know that?"

"Thank you," she says. Her Fae canines flash. "I know."

With Caer and Scott by my side, my powers magnify, buzzing through me at a chaotic speed.

"Do you feel that?"

"It's the joining of the trí cumhacht," Caer whispers, closing her eyes to absorb it.

"Wow," Scott says. "This takes power trip to a whole new level."

Together, the three of us could take on Breas, Witch Kensey, and the rest of the mindless swarms now surrounding the wall of fire.

"You took my servant and my prisoner," Breas growls at me from the other side of the flames.

"If you mean Ryan and Lizzie, they aren't your prize ponies. They're people."

He grins at me. His reaction is sickening. "They aren't people. They're werewolves."

"Tell me something I don't know."

"Did you neglect to realize what night it is?"

Something about his firm belief that I've made a serious miscalculation worries me. I glance up at the sky and see the full moon, almost at its apex, emerge from the clouds.

"The Oak Moon," he says. "A night of power and strength, especially on the night of the winter solstice."

Oh shit. How long had we been in the seomra de rúin? How long had I been knocked out after Alaric nearly killed me?

"Gigi," Alaric chokes beside me. "I can't stop it. Not on the solstice. I fought it as long as I could." His body twitches as he tries to combat the shift. "I won't be able to stop the change. I will kill you."

As if to confirm that fact, his green eyes flash to the yellow-gold of his wolf.

Panic removes my ability to breathe—and that's kinda important right now.

"I forgot about the full moon."

"We didn't," Witch Kensey says. She throws back her head and releases a howl, the primal call alerting every werewolf that reincarnated Brigit is here for the taking. It won't matter if they're from Maria and Declan's pack or a competing one. Their canines will drip saliva with the prospect of tasting my blood.

"Gigi, get out of here," Alaric groans. "You have to leave."

"Gigi," Maddie touches my arm. I leap away from him, terrified that he will kill me, but then I realize he doesn't have claws or teeth. The crystal . . .

Panic grips me once more as my hand shoots to my neck, remembering how Alaric had slashed at my necklace, sending the crystals flying all over the shrine room. But relief immediately washes over me because—thank the gods—the necklace is there, completely repaired. And I'm pretty sure I know who had taken the care to do that. I rip off the necklace and reach over Alaric's head. He tries to fight me off, but I'm determined to fasten it. The moment the crystals rest against his chest, his fangs retract, his green eyes return, and his claws disappear.

"You've done it," he gasps. "You've saved me. You saved us!" He crushes his lips to mine.

"Get your hands off of her," Breas shouts.

Alaric deepens the kiss instead.

"Enough," Witch Kensey snarls, and Alaric and I are ripped apart.

"The protections are breaking, Gigi," Scott says. "We have to get out of here. A portal would be great right about now."

Anna, Sam, Granda, and the rest of the coven nervously pace around the perimeter, chanting spells to keep the shields up.

I've only portal traveled with Scott.

"There are too many of us, and I won't leave them behind."

"No, there aren't. Join hands, everyone," Caer shouts.

The three of us take hands, further amplifying the power of the trí cumhacht. Alaric takes my other hand, Maddie takes his, and the rest of the coven quickly forms a large circle.

"Together," the three of us shout and a giant portal pulls us through. No need for shoving into this one.

"No!" Witch Kensey and Breas shout, but the sound grows more and more distant as the portal removes us from the danger. We've avoided death for the time being, but the storm is coming.

THE END

Continue reading for an excerpt from STORM MOON: THE GODDESS CHRONICLES BOOK 6 along with an excerpt from THRONE OF SILVER, the first book of the SILVER FAE SERIES

Reviews are like dance parties. Sometimes awkward, sometimes spastic, but someone has to get them started.

JOIN THE KOVEN

Read Clarissa and Carman's origin story, The Druids Sisters of the Gallicennial, FREE by signing up for K's Koven. Be the FIRST to find out about new releases from Best-Selling Author, K.B. Anne. PLUS, receive Newsletter Subscriber Only Bonus Content, insight on Celtic Mythology, Druids, Witches, Werewolves, and Magic, and so much more! Join K's Koven today!

ABOUT THE AUTHOR

Evil author person causing book hangovers since 2018. Known to erupt into malevolent laughter fits while she writes urban fantasy featuring fierce females, swoon worthy heroes who actually listen, and explosive action because everyone needs excitement in their lives.

She writes the best-selling urban fantasy series, *The Goddess Chronicles* and *The Silver Fae* Series. She has a thing for drool worthy wolf shapeshifters. Who doesn't?

She lives in Northeast PA with 3 goblins, a task master, 2 hell hound overlords, and 2 unicorns—though sadly they don't fart rainbow glitter. The Goddess Chronicles and Silver Fae Series are ready for your consumption. Warning: May cause book hangovers.

Visit her website for more information or to contact her at kbanne.com.

Contact info:
www.KBAnne.com
kim@kbanne.com

facebook.com/KBAnneWrite
twitter.com/KBAnneWrite
instagram.com/KBAnneWrite

The Goddess Chronicles (COMPLETE)

Wide Awake: The Goddess Chronicles Book 1

Blood Moon: The Goddess Chronicles Book 2

Dark Moon: The Goddess Chronicles Book 3

Shadow Moon: The Goddess Chronicles Book 4

Oak Moon: The Goddess Chronicles Book 5

Storm Moon: The Goddess Chronicles Book 6

The Goddess Chronicles Books 1-3 Boxset

The Goddess Chronicles Books 4-6 Boxset

The Silver Fae Series (COMPLETE)

Throne of Silver: Silver Fae 1

Silver Fae Hunter: Silver Fae 2

Heirs of Wings and Shadows: Silver Fae 3

Court of Wings and Shadows: Silver Fae 4

Crown of Flames: Silver Fae 5

STORM MOON: THE STARTLING CONCLUSION TO THE GODDESS CHRONICLES BOOK 6 EXCERPT

CHAPTER 1
FIRE IS FRIEND

Fire is friend. Or at least it seems to be at the moment. And so far it keeps Breas, the Fomorian Witch in the form of my nemesis Kensey, along with the rest of the mindless swarms at bay while I figure out what we should do next.

Alaric's green eyes find me. Thank the gods that the nightlock imbued crystal necklace I threw around his neck as the Oak Moon reached its apex kept him from turning into a werewolf and tearing out my throat. As a werewolf, he wasn't in complete control of his actions and would mourn killing me later—I'd mourn my death too, but still, stopping the change in the first place is much better.

"As long as this fire continues to burn we're trapped here," he says.

"I know, but I can't actually harm any living being, so until we figure out a Plan F.U., this is all I've got. At least I can create fire to keep our enemies out."

"There are many, but nothing compared to what Scott and I faced earlier," Caer says on the other side of me.

She's not lying. The battle in the Shadow Realm reminded

me of a Clash of the Titans-esque battle, with both Scott and Caer kicking ass and chopping off heads. Medusa's fighting skills got nothing on Caer, although Medusa's stony expression packs a weighty punch reminiscent of Balor. The two should have a staring contest and save the rest of us a lot of trouble.

"Any ideas what we should do next," Scott asks on the far side of Caer. He's wielding his own sword.

Breas's eyes fall to the handle of Scott's sword. I got up close and personal with Scott's sword during our seomra de ruin visit to the Shadow Realm, but I didn't notice his ruby encrusted handle. I swear I've seen that before.

Caer grips her handle beside me, and I realized why the handle looked familiar.

"Did you two go to Goibhniu, the god of weapon's armory and purchase matching swords? It's kinda adorable."

She arcs her blade through the air. "There is nothing adorable about a weapon that can slice an enemies head off."

Scott inches away from her, obviously familiar with her tendency to swing her sword around and probably not wanting to test their tenuous at best relationship—his words not mine. "The swords were wedding presents given to our godly forms. They return to us in every reincarnation and in time of need."

A werewolf lunges at the fire shield. As his body hits it, he cries out in pain as he gets launched backward his body aflame.

"We're in need of all the help we can get," Alaric says through clenched teeth, staring at the collapse wolf who hasn't moved since hitting the fire shield. Apparently, I can inadvertently hurt a living being if he or she were to propel themselves at one of my fire shields. I don't feel as satisfied that I hurt someone as I thought I would be.

I step over to him. "Can you retake command of your pack? Tell them to fight with us instead of against us? It would increase our odds."

More wolf eyes flash on the other side of the flames. "The whole packs here," he whispers.

"And they've brought friends," Scott says, "or your pack was much bigger than I thought it was."

Alaric crouches into a more combative lunge. "No, Declan's been recruiting."

My thoughts return to all the cells under the cavern "Or Carman's figured out a way to make more."

He stiffens. "She knows how to make them?"

My gaze slides over to Maddie. He ever so slightly raises his shoulders in a "I guess he doesn't know."

From what Maddie told me, Alaric bit and created most of their pack but apparently he was spelled and possesses no memory of it—which fit his claims when he first showed up in my room at Granda's in the middle of the night all those weeks ago and acted like he didn't know how he got there. His attraction to me probably made it easier for Carman to spell him.

But Alaric's been imprisoned with his father for weeks. He couldn't have been spelled to create new ones.

However, there was another child of Clayone available, and "recruits" could have been sent into the shrine via the tunnel.

"Alaric, did anyone come to visit your dad when you were in the shrine?"

He blinks in surprise at my question. "Not that I remember, and I don't remember smelling anyone either."

"Was Lizzie there the whole time? Did she ever leave?"

"As much as I'd love to have a sit down session to figure out how in purgatory's name there are so many werewolves, we need to figure out a plan of attack or an exit strategy because, wait… is that Kensey?" Scott stills as he stares at my nemesis but he's occasionally hookup. "She's a vessel for a Fomorian Witch. I always warned you she'd come back to bite you in the ass."

He shivers at the potential ramifications. "Well, whatever she is, she's cooking up some type of curse that no doubt will be nasty."

All our attention shifts to Kensey and indeed she's cooking up something especially sinister. "Carman's not the only one familiar with Maleficium."

Witch Kensey smiles at me, and I can just imagine her saying, "I am going to enjoy this." There are an exceptional scary number of similarities between the two—that's probably what attracted Breas to Kensey in the first place.

"What should we do?" Scott says shifting from foot to foot. "I'm good, but I'm not too keen on discovering how well Moralltach blocks curses."

"You named your sword?" Boys with their toys.

"Swords of honor all have names. Mine is Freagarach," Caer growls, her Fae canines flashing. "I say let's fight."

The last time Scott and I fought a crazed Maleficium witch, Dad and Calliope died in the crossfire. Tonight, we've already lost Gallean and Clarissa. I can't bear for anyone else to lose their life or risk injury.

Without discussing it with anyone without asking permission, I imagine a portal that will fit everyone including all of Granda's coven. One appears in front of me. "Everyone join hands!" I yell, and we do.

"No!!!!" roars Kensey witch blasting the fire shield to bits, but she's too late, because everyone within the shield disappears into the portal.

To keep reading, grab your copy of
Storm Moon: The Goddess Chronicles Book 6

Keep reading for an excerpt of
Throne of Silver: Silver Fae Book 1

THRONE OF SILVER: SILVER FAE SERIES BOOK 1 EXCERPT

CHAPTER 1

Dive in.

That was the advice the swim team captain gave me when I gingerly dipped my toe in the pool at my first 5:30 a.m. swim practice three years ago. You see, the cold shocks your body into action. Stroke after stroke, you concentrate on your breathing, and the angle of your arms as they reach and pull through the water, and the height and depth of your kick, rather than on the freezing temperatures—at least that's the idea anyway.

Dive in.

I took that advice to heart. Made it my life's mantra, really.

So, when Sami texted me about a summer fellowship at Trevnor University's Leadership Academy, I begged her to pick me up an application. I couldn't think of a better way to spend June, July, and August than adding Summer Fellowship to my Georgetown application. My early acceptance was all but guaranteed.

But the entrance exam was tomorrow, at the tail end of

my post-season training for States, and in the midst of planning prom, Spring Fling, and our junior class trip, plus track started Monday.

Dive in.

My mantra sometimes got me in over my head.

CHAPTER 2

Laughter exploded around me as I hurried through the school's front entrance. Over by the water fountain, four seniors played Hacky Sack while an audience of giggly underclassmen watched, making noises accentuated with rounded oohs and angled aahs. They all probably went to last night's basketball game too—the lucky bastards. While I discussed table linens and canapés with hotel managers, they got to watch the Webster Titans trounce the Bay Cardinals, 90-40.

Sometimes I hated these classmates of mine.

I mean *really* hated them.

None of them had two hours of swim practice this morning. None of them had two meetings during school, another meeting after school, followed by two more hours of swim practice. None of them had a To Do list so complicated and involved, even I knew it wouldn't be completed until after graduation.

Sometimes I wondered what it would be like not to worry about tomorrow, or next week, or next year. To live in the moment and just *be*.

A long stream of water hit me square on the nose.

Or not...

Shocked gasps ping-ponged through the ten-foot wide, locker-lined hallway, followed by an awkward, collective silence.

My body flickered—it had been doing that a lot lately especially when I got mad or annoyed about something. It felt like ocean waves slamming against my chest, and no matter how strong a swimmer I was, sometimes the big ones knocked me on my ass even when I was only knee deep.

I took a few deep breaths to calm myself. Thankfully, the flickering stopped. I was never standing in front of a mirror when it happened so I didn't know if the flickering was something other people saw or it was just in my head—which concerned me on a number of levels, but I couldn't worry about any of that right now. Someone needed to be punished for their crime.

I tracked the gaze of the surprised onlookers. My assailant, an underclassman with an unsteady grip on a green squirt gun, shook in his red Nike sneakers. I wiped my face and flicked the water in his direction. The droplets soared through the air and landed on his flushed, round cheeks. To his credit, he took it like a man, but unfortunately for him, he became the target of the dark, foul mood that descended upon me the moment I stepped into school.

"Don't you have a place you need to be?"

"Y...yes, sssorry Starrrr," he said, adding an overflowing consonant stream in the already crowded hallway. I narrowed my eyes. He tossed the squirt gun into the garbage can and sprinted away, red Nikes and all. When the plastic toy landed at the bottom of the can, it was as if someone hit play and all the students returned to their regularly non-scheduled lives.

Yep, today, I *definitely* hated them.

I stomped through the crowds, throwing the occasional elbow and the well-directed shove, because evidently, I was still the only one who needed to be somewhere.

Frank's buzzed head towered over the sea of students. I caught a glimpse of tight red ringlets by his side and understood why he didn't wait for me after practice.

He glanced down the crowded hall. A broad smile crossed his face the moment he saw me. One icy vein thawed. "Hey Starr," he said, then winked at the redhead. "I'll see *you* later."

"Bye Frankie," she replied, smiling like she just won the boyfriend sweepstakes. Frank was the total package—tall, dark, handsome with the brains and personality to match, but he wouldn't date Little Red long enough for her to find out. He went through girls faster than he swam the fifty, and he held the school record in that.

I frowned at him. "Frankie?"

He shrugged.

I spun my combination into my locker. "She already has a nickname for you?"

He smirked.

I tried my combo again, but my locker refused to cooperate. It was like it wanted to add further insult to injury.

At least in this case, I could cause bodily harm to it without being frowned upon. I kicked the base of the locker since my foul mood hadn't completely lifted and kicking metal seemed like a productive means to releasing frustration. Plus I didn't know what was up with the whole body flickering thing. I wasn't even sure if I wanted to mention it to my best friend.

Frank rested his hands on my shoulders and guided me to the side. He hit the locker just below the locking mechanism, and it popped open. He smiled as he rested against the locker next to mine. "When you got it, you got it."

I rolled my eyes.

"You know, I'm considered quite a prince to every girl in this school but…" He zeroed in a finger on my nose.

I swatted it away. "I know how charming you can be. The entire female population of Roger G. Webster High knows how charming you can be."

He closed the distance between us. "I can't help it if girls find me irresistible, but my dating days would come to an end if you went out with me."

Most girls would love the attention Frank gave me. *Most* girls would grow red-faced and faint if they heard half the come-ons he practiced on me. *Most* girls haven't been best friends with him since he was a short, obnoxious, hormone-ridden, scrawny seventh grader who wore ratty yellow Sponge Bob t-shirts and couldn't get a date to save his life.

I shoved him into class. "Get a grip."

To keep reading, grab your copy of
Throne of Silver, Silver Fae Book 1